IN THE BEGINNING

THERE WAS

LAUGHTER

By Abe Kleiman

This book is a work of fiction. Places, events, and situations in this story are purely fictional. Any resemblance to actual persons, living or dead, is coincidental.

© 2004 by Abe Kleiman. All rights reserved.

No part of this book may be reproduced, stored in a retrieval system, or transmitted by any means, electronic, mechanical, photocopying, recording, or otherwise, without written permission from the author.

ISBN: 1-4107-1927-8 (e-book)
ISBN: 1-4107-1928-6 (Paperback)

Library of Congress Control Number: 2003090817

This book is printed on acid free paper.

Printed in the United States of America
Bloomington, IN

1stBooks – rev. 01/29/04

In the Beginning There Was Laughter

SPECIAL THANKS

Special thanks to my wife, Elaine Kleiman, for her many hours reviewing my written story and drawings (sometimes at two a.m.) and for assisting me from beginning to end. I would like to thank my daughter, Judy Bloom, for reviewing my story and cartoons. Thank you to Kristen Foster, who guided me through the Internet and handled many of the details that helped me in completing this book.

Thank you Maxine and Jack Halabe for editing the second galley.

You may find that many cartoons were completed at an early date. We decided they should be included to provide the reader a good understanding of my humor in the good old days. This was my "early period." You can also take note of the changes in cartoon styles over a fifty-year period. Enjoy!

Abe Kleiman

Dedicated to
my grandchildren
Jacob, Madelyn, Raphaela and Xander

In the Beginning There Was Laughter

Cartoons! Cartoons! Cartoons!

I have spent the better part of my life playing second fiddle to cartoons.

My husband is a cartoonist. Do you know what it is like to live with a cartoonist? You cannot even begin to imagine. Everything you say and do turns into a cartoon. Your hairdo, your new outfit, your bathing suit, your thoughts, animals, babies, construction sites, athletic games, exercising, all become subjects for cartoons.

Nothing is sacred. Events in your life such as weddings, funerals, birth of children, and religious services are not exempt.

I have been awakened at three a.m. because "the cartoonist" thought of something funny and is afraid he will forget it if he does not share it with me. I have been asked, "What did I tell you about that cartoon I wanted to draw when we were at the movies last week? Can't you remember?"

It's not the cartoonist's fault. He has a weird perspective of the world. He sees things from a different slant. He is a writer who sees his words in pictures and situations with a sense of humor peculiar to him. His view can be fantasy, enlightening, political, dreamlike, or realistic but always drawn in a way to entertain the viewer.

So, finally, these cartoons have been assembled and maybe after all these years our lives can get back to being "normal" if there is such a thing.

Elaine M. Kleiman

Abe Kleiman

In the Beginning There Was Laughter

Why do I look at the funny side? As far as I'm concerned, humor is everywhere, but you must focus on it in everyday circumstances. For example, I am sitting at the pool in Longboat Key, Florida, with friends and enjoying a typical discussion about everyday matters. I happen to be looking north on the key because of sounds and noises. I am viewing the construction of a five-story condominium, the basic structure with concrete pillars and structural frames, with scaffolding up to the third floor. What catches my eye is this enormous crane about 70 feet high maneuvering and finally lifting a (honey bucket) portable toilet now dangling on a hook beneath this towering structure. The imagination kicks in. What if the portable toilet were being used? Yes, this situation appears in one of my cartoons. Throughout my life I get a view of things that could happen in a normal day that could be bizarre or somewhat different with a little twist. A normal situation could become hilarious. I could be flying on a commercial jet and interpret the minimizing of services in a funny way or when you go into their toilet and flush and hear that powerful suction sound … yes, this also appears in my cartoons.

Where did all this begin?

I guess it all began with my parents and my humble beginnings. We were on the poor side by today's standards and middle class by my past standards. Born in 1926, the Depression was a big factor in our lives and my parents looked at saving money at any cost. For example, I was born at home and had my tonsils removed at home. So, at age 57 when I appeared at Tuft's University Hospital in Boston for an examination before surgery, the nurse gave me some forms to fill out. It required information about previous hospital stays, which I left blank. Needless to say, the nurse promptly questioned me. "Mr. Kleiman, you did not mention the hospitals you must have been in, your birth or other hospital stays. Please complete the form." "But nurse! I have never stayed in a hospital!" "Really?" "Yes, really!" "You see my parents were very stringent with money, or was it cheap?" Anyway, in those days, hospitalization was "in the mind of the beholder." In the Great Depression, people fixed their minds on saving every penny they could lay their hands on and developed very frugal habits. These habits disappeared after the Depression. So what is so funny about the Great Depression? My mother would move her family of four about every three years. I felt like an overdone traveler. Why did we move so often? The word was "concession." This meant every time we moved the landlord gave us one free month's rent and a free paint job. Our rent was twenty-eight dollars a month. Over the years I recall families moving into trailer camps and renting mobile homes on fixed pieces of property and there goes my imagination. I picture a family driving away in a rented mobile home, and in hot pursuit is the landlord. They are renters looking out their window yelling to the father who is driving the mobile home, "Faster, faster, they are catching up to us." Any day's normal happenings can be changed into humor with a little imagination. Everyday happenings can become bizarre, funny, and side splitting.

My father was a perfect example of humor. He was very quiet but opinionated and either liked you or disliked you and no in-between. He disliked my aunt, who lived with us for many years before she married. This was a sacrifice for my mother. She did not want my aunt to live alone. I remember years later, after her marriage, my aunt came to visit us, this one time. One Friday evening my father is tinkering around the house and the doorbell rings. Mother had invited my aunt and uncle over. Instantly my father sits down in his favorite lounge chair and within a flash he is snoring with his mouth open wide. In walks my aunt and uncle. Mother says, "Philip is sleeping, walk softly into the kitchen. I have coffee and cake ready." Two hours pass and my aunt and uncle start to leave softly passing my father (Philip) in his comfortable lounge chair still heavily snoring away. As the door closed, at the speed of lightning my father stands up and says, "Any cake and coffee left?"

A funny thing happened to me when I fell on my face.

You heard it correctly. There we are. My wife and a friend and I are going on a tour of a winery in the state of Washington. I have had

In the Beginning There Was Laughter

a physical problem walking and use a cane especially while on a tour or walking through a mall. This time I am walking up the concrete steps to the winery anticipating the fine taste of wine at the wine tasting counter. Within a flash I fall instantly like rock onto the hard concrete pavement. The sound of my body falling forward on my stomach resounds through the air. Instantly people from all around me hurry to my side to assist me with open arms offering to lift me to my feet. At that moment the cell phone on my belt rings. I quickly reach for it with my right hand and hold it up in a stop motion and say to the concerned crowd, "Hold it please. I have a call." I would say that is instant humor without any thought or imagination. Just a natural happening.

Other Gems of Happenings:

Years ago I had made an appointment to meet a friend of mine so we could proceed to see a movie together. This was before cell phones existed. The instructions were to meet in front of a well-known diner on Sunrise Highway in Lynbrook, New York, at seven p.m. sharp. I arrived at the appointed location and to my surprise there was a great big hole in the ground. No diner and no friend. That diner had been there as long as I could remember. We never got together that evening. Instant humor happens to all of us. The idea is to remember it and recognize it for what it is, a gem of humor.

Simple things like poetry, which we all hear from time to time, can ring out with humor. This simple poem I heard many years ago, and I can still remember:

A little bear sleeps in his little bearskin;
He is very warm I am told.
Last night I slept in my little bare skin
And caught a heck of a cold.

A Matter of Language Misinterpretation:

My mother and dad emigrated from Russia and Romania. Needless to say, we misunderstood each other on many occasions.

Abe Kleiman

My wife and I moved into our new home in New York and introduced ourselves to our neighbors. Understand my parents come from a Jewish background and all their friends, relatives and acquaintances and people in their community are mostly Jewish with Jewish-sounding names. In many instances people would eventually Americanize their names. As it happened our new neighbors names are May and Sam Wong; yes, you guessed it, they are Chinese.

My mother calls excitedly wanting to know if we have met our new neighbors and, "As matter of fact," I respond, "Yes!" And my mother asks what are their names and I respond that their names are May and Sam Wong. Then there is a momentary pause and my mother says, "They must have changed their name from Weiner and they are probably Jewish." That broke me up, but with a straight face and casual response I say, "But they don't look Jewish."

I was born at the right time.

I was drafted into the army in 1945 during World War II, which was a time humor would be hard to find. This was a time when many lives were lost. I went through basic training in Florida in the sweltering heat, 20-mile hikes and the most extreme negative situations especially during "bivouac." This was an ordeal for us poor infantry soldiers experiencing basic training going out into the open fields of the bowels of Florida. This environment and exposure in the open wilderness included torrential rains, mud, muck and mire and tripping over one of the most poisonous snakes, the coral snake. There were no toilets, showers or bathtubs. Approaching a large lake one day I quickly strip down to my birthday suit leaving my GI clothes, knapsack, shovel, rolled half tent, canteen, rifle, ammunition, a week's supply of rations and last but not least my bayonet. The water is cool and refreshing but my luck comes to an abrupt end. On the bank of the lake from nowhere appears this large black wild pig (Florida is loaded with them). It starts smelling my knapsack and in an eyewink this pig is tearing away smelling out the food. Almost everything I had left neatly on the bank of the lake is being shredded and torn apart. I quickly move toward my possessions and that pig will not let up. I yell and it squeals. In desperation to save my life's sustenance I grab the bayonet, removing the blade from the sheath. I throw the bayonet at the pig because it could mean my survival. The blade of the bayonet penetrates the pig and I hear the loudest squeal from the pig and in a flash it is gone and so is my bayonet. Back at the camp supply depot I report the loss to the supply sergeant and the next thing I know I am being charged $18 for losing my bayonet. Now it's a laugh but in those days it was devastating.

Unintentional Funny Situations

A friend of ours, who started losing his hair in his early years, appeared one day with an absolutely good looking toupee. We became accustomed to this toupee over the years. We are gathered together one evening at his parent's home. After awhile his mother approaches him and says, "Al, I do not like the way you part your hair." We look at each other and roar with laughter. Obviously, his mother has forgotten after so many years that he is bald.

Abe Kleiman

Mother and I. In the days before "weight watchers."

WHY I DECIDED TO WRITE THIS BOOK.
(Growing Up)

I am a 75-year-old Jewish boy from the Bronx, NY. I am a World War II veteran who, hopefully, can think, write and draw cartoons. In the beginning, I thought that I would be one of the best cartoonists ever. But in the beginning I didn't have any concept of supporting myself and possibly increasing my wealth. Back then, my youthful brain told me I would sell my cartoons immediately if not sooner. This never happened. Not "never" - I have sold cartoons and comic strip ideas from the early days after returning from my overseas duty and being discharged from army service. I have sold cartoons professionally to many magazines including New York Magazine, Boys Life, Sports Life, Colliers, and comic strip ideas for Little Audrey.

I come from a family that included an overweight mother who originated from Kiev, Russia, and a quiet, introverted father with a fantastic sense of humor. Both parents were not more than five feet tall, although my father proclaimed and advertised his height as five feet two inches. My hunch always was that included his cigar, which was continually part of his dress either in his hand or mouth. My mother was always the homemaker and a fabulous cook. Little did we know that Jewish cooking preceded the holocaust in causing the early deaths of so many. Our diets included large portions of *Grievena* (fried chicken skin) and onions and we kept the chicken fat and smeared it over bread as an appetizer. Salads were considered similar to grass and my folks ate them only on rare occasions. At an early age I seemed to possess an angelic face with big kindly eyes. Although from my sister's perspective it was the "kiss of death." My sister is two years older than I and despised me. If the milk bottle crashed on the floor, splattering milk and glass all over the kitchen, my mother would seek us out. Of course neither my sister nor I could be found in the immediate area. My mother could pack a mean whack and I had experienced contact with a rolling pin, so when asked I would reply, "Who, me?" And my innocence would be expressed and advertised over my face like a neon sign. My sister never had a chance. My mother would call *Chaika* (her Yiddish name) and all hell would break loose resulting in my sister having to clean up. My sister was given the English name, Aida, which we are all familiar with as the name of a famous opera. Throughout my life I wondered how did my sister ever get the name Aida? My father and mother never went to or listened to opera.

Among my close family members was my Aunt Elsie, who, not surprisingly, ate the same food we did resulting in her forming a structure resembling Yogi Berra, but before Yogi she resembled a fire hydrant. Because of this, I assumed she would never marry, but my mother, who could sell refrigerators to Eskimos, succeeded in what is called in Yiddish a *Shidoch*: a match with a wealthy (by our standards) gentleman from upstate New York. Aunt Elsie would like to hold me in her lap and squeeze me into a love hold. I did not like to be held and expressed myself physically. The results were black and blue knees for my aunt from the heavy leather shoes I wore.

A marked characteristic of those times after the crash of 1929 was that most people were frugal and in most families every nickel spent had to be discussed with the family. My parents and aunt and uncle shared this mentality. Although my aunt and uncle lived very comfortably and spent weeks and months on Florida vacations, there was a mental block on any and all spending. One year my wife and I and another couple went to Florida for two weeks. It dawned on me that my aunt and uncle were in this hotel in Florida and I thought it would be a good idea to call them. However my sadistic brain took command. Picking up the phone from our hotel room I dialed their number. My aunt answered the phone and after she said, "Hello," I placed my hand on my nose trying to imitate an operator and said, "I have a collect call from Mr. Abe Kleiman; will you accept the charges?" Complete silence on the other end. Finally after a minute or two I heard my aunt's voice say, "Jack, it's for you." Silence again. Then my aunt said, "Sorry but he is on the toilet. Please call again in twenty minutes."

We were visiting someone at Saint Joseph's Hospital in Far Rockaway, New York. Upon entering the hospital, standing in front of us was a large statue of a figure that may have represented Saint

In the Beginning There Was Laughter

Joseph. The statue was chunky with broad shoulders. My daughter, Judy, who was three years old, took one look at the statue and said, " Why do they have a statue of Aunt Elsie here?"

Humor Everywhere, Even in the Obituaries

First let me say that obituaries give news and details of a loved one's death. I read them to observe and wonder how an individual lived, especially his or her past contributions. The famous ones pique my curiosity about what their contribution or detraction was in life. Obituaries are straightforward, and if you can catch some humor, it will be very humorous and much funnier than you think. For example, this woman died and, as I read, her claim to fame was that she was Senator Strom Thurman's babysitter. That is mind-boggling and funny. He is 99 years old and she died at age 109 and voted for him in every election including 1996. Then there was Moe Greenglass who died at the age of 84 and had an appetizing store that was very successful. He was given the title, "The Sturgeon King." He developed a clientele of the rich and famous all over the world who marveled at the taste of his smoked fish and lox. He was loyal to his customers and his customers to him. Jascha Heifetz (the most famous and prominent violinist of his time) called and asked him to ship him a pound of sliced lox as soon as possible and Moe asked, "Are you really Jascha Heifetz on the phone?" Then to make sure he wasn't an impostor, Moe asked the famous celebrity to play for him over the phone and he did. The lox was shipped Fedex pronto!

How I Ended World War II

My service in the army started February 15th, 1945. Fort Dix, New Jersey, was the farthest I had been away from home. Then we proceeded to Camp Blanding, Florida, which was the opposite of Miami Beach. A subtitle for camp was "the hell hole of the universe." Twenty-mile hikes in quick time cadence toughened me up. Camping or "bivouacking" was an experience. At night I teamed up with another "buddy" and we put up a tent for sleeping consisting of two halves of canvas assembled and staked to the ground with rope and wood poles. Two thirty a.m. we floated out of our tent with a rush of water. No one told us not to bed down in a dry ravine. As if I wasn't toughened up enough, technically World War II in Europe was over. So, what to do with an eighteen-year-old reserve infantryman private? They sent me to Camp Rucker, Alabama. Now, I had experience because in Florida I used to march 20 miles under intensive heat and humidity with a full backpack. Here at Camp Rucker I could improve on that to maybe 30 miles. Here they promoted me to acting sergeant. This is called advancement. Well, not really: the stripes were on a black band that was placed around the arm and at the end of the day the band came off and I became a full-blown private again. My most life-threatening experience happened here in good old Camp Rucker. One exercise in training was how to properly throw a live hand grenade. A hand grenade looks like a little pineapple with a handle on the side. You run into this ditch, pull this ring, which has a stem on the end of it; the handle pops off and you throw the grenade over the mound of dirt in front of you and be sure to lie down as close to the earth as possible. I was well into the earth, my eyes full of and my mouth breathing dirt. Now, you must wait four seconds and then you should hear a loud burst or explosion. The reason that you lay low is to avoid any shrapnel, which could be dangerous to your health. After four seconds nothing happened; ten minutes later a voice from behind ordered me to move because behind me was the whole battalion of infantry men on the same exercise. It's like being a slow golfer on a golf course holding up the golfer behind you. Looking at my hand I noticed the stem from the grenade was missing from the ring. The stem was locked in the grenade. This is like playing Russian roulette. A half an hour later the yelling and cursing behind me increased to a thunderous pitch. Peering behind me I could hear this noise but no one was standing. "Get your ass out of here; you are holding up this exercise." I felt like a mole in a hole crawling back.

Next I recall boarding a troop train heading for the West Coast. I had never before experienced traveling through our beautiful country, making stops in major towns and cities. Ah yes, I remember White Fish, Montana in the middle of summer, exiting the train for some exercise for half an hour. It was so cold I could see my own breath. One week later we debarked from our train and settled into a camp,

In the Beginning There Was Laughter

which was to prepare us for overseas duty. In the meantime we had to perform the duties before us. I was assigned to guard German prisoners of war. I called them Nazis, and because I understood Yiddish and could understand a lot of German, I told the prisoners around me that I killed many Germans during the war but it was not my fault because I was only following orders. Remember, I had the M-I rifle and this fabricated story gained me a lot of polite Germans who smiled and always asked how my day was.

I was not in the best of moods at this time in my life. Although the war was over I did not like the fact that shortly we were headed for overseas service and this probably meant that we were replacing those who had actually experienced combat. I was basically wondering about the unknown and how long it would be before I would return to my family and friends. On the bulletin board was posted a hotline: that Friday night would be a social event with gals from around our northern California camp arriving at eight p.m.

I decided to attend, as did most of the soldiers at the base. Sure enough I hit pay dirt. This very friendly, sexy-looking smiling gal came right on to me. My mood quickly changed and after a wonderful evening I was flabbergasted when I was invited to spend a weekend at this gorgeous gal's home. This was a spur of the moment situation and I was able to get a weekend pass. I packed a light bag and was ready to leave when on the loudspeaker system a commanding voice stated that all leaves were canceled because we had immediate orders to ship out the next day for overseas duty. All this happened that Friday evening. I was devastated and this gal who was so gracious and friendly, I am certain, felt the same. We exchanged addresses and telephone numbers and that was the end of our relationship.

I clearly remember that departure as if it were yesterday. The name of the ship was the SS Leonard Wood. As we boarded ship a band played a popular tune called "Sentimental Journey." The lyrics ended with "Going to take a sentimental journey, sentimental journey home." It was the saddest song and the saddest day of my life.

No one sat around in this army. You had to work at something such as swabbing decks, or KP (kitchen police). They found work for

Abe Kleiman

us that our parents wouldn't dare suggest, such as cleaning and scrubbing down the bathrooms. So when an announcement over the PA system was heard I quickly volunteered. "If there are any butchers aboard this vessel please report to the kitchen." I arrived at the kitchen within five minutes at what I would estimate to be the speed of lightning.

Our scheduled trip would be at least two weeks. Our destination was the Philippine Islands, with one stop on the way in the Hawaiian Islands. Most important we would receive only two meals per day. That was down from three meals at home and an open refrigerator. So I became an instant butcher. This was my desperate attempt at avoiding starvation and it worked. Every morning I reported to the kitchen at 4:30 a.m. and was handed a meat cleaver and stationed over a wood butcher block. They handed me a whole side of pork and, peering over my shoulder at the next butcher, I tried to imitate his motions with the meat cleaver. After decimating four sides of pork I was demoted to forming hamburger patties, which proved to be successful. I learned to walk in and out of the freezer cabinet often because I discovered ice cream sandwiches by the thousands among other goodies. This ship had 10,000 mouths to feed and *someone* had to do it. My job ended daily at 12:30 p.m. And from all appearances I looked like I gained a lot of weight. However, unbeknown to the ship's managing officers, I had hidden an assortment of food, which was distributed among my close friends with whom I developed lasting serious friendships. The two weeks abruptly ended upon our arrival in the Philippine Islands. Remember, we had received only two meals a day. Some of our compatriots started a bidding war for the food that I had sneaked out of the kitchen. If I had been on the ship another two weeks, this butcher could have purchased the boat. We disembarked from the army troop ship on a very hot and humid day. The army has a saying that was relevant throughout my days in service: "Hurry up and wait." We stood in this hot and sweltering sun for hours. But the time had come when many of the troops waiting on this beach and I among them had to go to the bathroom. We all take for granted that wherever we are a bathroom is accessible. The U.S. Army had taken care of the situation. On the beach was what looked like a giant coffin, a rectangular configuration made of wood. On the top surface were six holes spaced evenly about 12 inches in diameter. The box was placed over an approximately six-foot deep rectangular

In the Beginning There Was Laughter

hole in the ground, simply designed to accommodate GI's when we had a sudden urge. My turn came, and I pulled down my trousers and sat bare-assed on this hole with five other GI's alongside of me and with a line of men waiting as far as the eye could see. Parading in front of us were about eight Filipino native women carrying open boxes and wearing little red bandannas on their heads. They stopped and placed the open boxes in front of us and pitched a sale. "Hey, Joe, want to buy banana?" The guy next to me reaches into his pants pocket while defecating and says, "Give me six of those bananas. How much?" The guy on the next seat says, "Hey, Frank, don't buy that; it makes you shit and there is a big line out there."

By the time things settled down, I found myself in an outfit consisting of 300 men in a town on the Philippine Island of Luzon. The town or city was called Batangas. The US Army transferred me to an army base on the shores of Batangas and we operated and maintained boats and other watercraft. What happened to the Navy? Very big mistake! About 200 18- and 19-year-old kids arrived at this base whose intent was to relieve the army veterans of World War II who were skilled at operating and maintaining harbor craft. The base consisted of a huge Quonset hut (a building constructed of corrugated metal walls with a round roof like a letter U in reverse). The ages of army personnel were from approximately 25 to late 30s. I would call a guy of 35 years of age, "Pops"; can you imagine how that could be?

Our camp was behind this very large Catholic Church in back of which was a graveyard. However, I did not know it was a graveyard until I tripped over this skull protruding through the ground. This happened after a heavy tropical rainstorm, which occured there almost every day. Our floor consisted of mud that formed in our ten-men tents. Outside the tents I observed water flowing and puddles throughout the camp streets.

The cemetery extended about 60 yards and our camp was built behind the graveyard. They cleared an area of heavy plant and tree growth and simply built ten-men tents out to an area of over 100 yards by 50 yards. Behind that was the maintenance and repair shop at the water's edge and about fifty LCMs and LCVPs, which basically were landing craft used for landing troops and supplies

The Army did give us electricity. Our camp had two generators. I immediately became the camp electrician because an elderly gentleman of 36 with whom I had become friendly offered me his job as the camp electrician. Now it seems that John Colucci was going home on points. The point system was invoked by the army to allow the veterans to return home and be replaced by us kids. However, you must remember that we had no experience, besides playing stickball in the streets of New York or baseball in the parks.

Three quarters of the army replacements were from the Deep South and we had a language barrier. Therefore we had two army units and I replaced an individual who spoke English.

John originated from Rockaway Beach and I lived in Rockaway Beach but at the other end. Rockway is located in the borough of Queens, New York City. I would receive packages from home consisting mainly of large kosher salami and John received Italian salami and other items which we shared with each other. John was a very responsible individual and attempted to teach me the workings of generating electricity. Firstly we had two electric generators. One was an AC generator powered by gasoline and the other was a DC generator powered by diesel oil. The question arose as to why we needed two generators. It seemed that during the daylight the AC generator was the first choice. It did not have the power to generate electricity in the evening, so at 5 p.m. I would shut down the AC generator and power up the DC generator. John also developed a relationship with the priests and nuns. The Christmas holidays were approaching and he would be leaving shortly. He asked me to wire up the church for services. John was a very friendly guy and unbeknownst to me had electrified many homes in the native community around us, charging them for services. When John left I inherited a miniature electric utility company. The trouble began among the many appliances requiring electricity.

In the Beginning There Was Laughter

U.S. Army harbor craft unit in Batangas, Philippines.

Abe Kleiman

We had secured a transmitter and receiver and PA system powered by a Halicrafter set. In those days that was the state of the art system. Throughout the day we played all the popular records on the PA and this interlude of music lifted our spirits. Now this Halicrafter set was our gem but at five p.m. the AC generator was manually shut down. When I was not on base I would give instructions to some of the people in my unit to shut down the AC generator and turn on the DC generator. Now you may ask, what's the big deal? The Halicrafter set, which was valued at four hundred dollars, had a built in transformer. In the States, everything was powered by AC electricity. The DC generator would burn out the transformer and that would be the end of our PA system. There were no replacement parts. At 5 p.m. it would become dark. The AC generator, as I said, could not supply enough power to support the lights at the base.

I would leave the base on many occasions and my trustworthy people would switch off the Halicraftor PA system then shut down the AC generator and switch on the DC generator. Two miles down the road was our PX, which was a restful place for stressed out GIs. It was as close as you could get to the States because it had a wide assortment of products that you could purchase. The PX was as close as you could get to a supermarket, candy store, and lounge. While sitting comfortably at 5:45 p.m. enjoying a coke my name was blasted on the PA system: "Abe Kleiman return to base. This is an emergency." I could not drive, but a few of my comrades were available to take me and I got back to base. The first thing I observed was smoke coming from one of the tents. It was the tent that contained the Halicrafter set. It was filled with thick billowing smoke and the noxious smell that signaled the end of our Halicrafter set. I was distraught and devastated. No one had switched off the Halicrafter set as they had been instructed to do. They had switched off the AC generator and switched on the DC generator only because the lights would not work. At 6:30 p.m. in that tent with the heavy smoldering noxious billowing smoke sat six soldiers doing their jobs. They were playing poker choking in chorus. Jeb said, "How can you say you have aces over queens; I can't see them." I could not imagine how they stayed alive in that tent.

I was confronted by a blackened, greasy-looking highest-ranking officer in our battalion the 301 Harbor Craft. We called him Helen because he was very effeminate and many thought of him as being homosexual, which could not be determined. As I approached with a sad sympathetic look on my face, he became very emotional almost to the point of hysteria. To the noxious odors and billowing smoke was now added sparks and arcing of electricity; Helen looked like a well-roasted chicken. He was almost incoherent. Helen had kept to himself and was not informed of our procedures. The troops had not shut down the AC generator at five p.m. The lights went on, as I mentioned, which overloaded our AC generator causing it to burn out. Now we were left with one diesel generator and no means to broadcast music announcements and important communications through our camp.

There remained a few veterans among us who informed us of a very special place in midtown Manila that contained supplies of everything from bulldozers to kitchen utensils. All we needed was a requisition paper and a two and a half ton truck. At five, one morning, four of us clambered aboard the truck. We lumbered down a road heading north until by hit or miss we came to a gate guarded by a very official looking soldier. We were almost shitting in our pants; what if they discovered our forged papers that were signed by ourselves and what if they did not have the Halicrafter set and generator?

After showing our papers the gate opened and we entered a vast area of wooden crates so high and as far as the eye could see. I thought I was back home in the Bronx, where tenement buildings rose five to six stories high, each building flush against each other until a street separated them. We drove down one street and met one live person who did not know where AC generators could be found. But, luckily, we were informed as to the street at which the Halicrafter sets could be found. After finding them we removed four, placed them in our truck and changed the numbers on our requisition form. This was important because in my total stay at the base we burnt out six Halicrafter sets and had to come back for more. Looking high and low in this enormous supply depot it turned out that amongst all the troops at this base everyone we met were replacements, meaning, "I don't know."

On the way back to base we were all not exactly happy. The entertainment center cannot operate without electricity. One of the guys with a long memory recalled that one of the veterans left base

Abe Kleiman

illegally, married a native gal and somehow got himself a generator which he proudly displayed under a stilted house with a native thatched roof having interwoven palm leaves for walls.

At three, one morning four quietly moving personnel from our battalion approached the area of the veteran's home and found the AC generator. The thatched huts were simply built on four wood posts about eight to ten feet off the ground to prevent jungle animals from coming in looking for a meal. So, it was easy to eye ball the generator. With stealth we moved the generator, which was built on four sturdy rubber tires that made it portable. Quietly we disconnected the wires leading down to the generator and rolled it away in the dead of night. Driving back to base we were wondering if Mr. Retired Veteran could figure out where his generator had gone.

We came back to base conquering heroes. Life went back to normal with records spinning music through the PA systems speakers and announcements by commanding personnel and guys hamming up the airways. There had also been urgency in completing the PA system problem because it was just before Christmas.

I was not a happy trooper. Although John Colucci had given me a quick education about running a generator and wiring the camp area and tents, I had one incident I vividly recall wiring a newly installed tent. There were flaps on top of each side of the tent. That was one way to bring wiring into a tent and string it across its length. My work force consisted of a group of Japanese prisoners of war who were camped adjacent to our camp and a group of Filipino laborers. I requested them to switch off the generator while I was wiring the tent. Climbing a 12-foot ladder I climbed through the vent flaps, stretching to reach the wire secured from a pole leading from the generator. As I was stripping the insulation from the wire with my metal cutting tool, *POW*, you guessed it, I was hit with a tremendous jolt and went flying off the top of the ladder. Gravity did the rest. I just tore through the canvas fabric like a knife. The tent and I hit the ground. Some guys were in the tent waiting for the lights to go on but they were in for a "dark" surprise. Fortunately I was not injured, just shocked. This incident was just a preliminary to a master problem. Christmas was coming up fast and John Colucci had planned to electrify the church and set up an amplifying system before our government sent him home. I promised him that I would do the job. I met with Father

In the Beginning There Was Laughter

Thomas and was introduced to all the nuns, priests, lay people and workers.

Me, Japanese prisoner
of war and an army buddy.

Abe Kleiman

I counted 18 people associated with the church. They were part of a Spanish order. When I told Father Thomas that John Colucci had asked me to electrify the church for Christmas he gave me a broad smile and shook my hand very expressively. Looking around the church, which I assumed had been built in the early 1900s, I saw that it was in very poor condition. My first negative thoughts were regarding the interior. The ceiling was over forty feet high. However, being an 18-year-old replacement my little brain said "no sweat."

With my crew - native Filipino's and a hand picked crew of Japanese war prisoners - we had 28 men. We scaled the walls and placed the wires. Studying the model of wiring of our base we completed the job in three days and the generator switch went on. Much to our surprise, a short circuit occurred. The Generator was imediately turned off. Luckily the generator did not burn out. This 18-year-old had screwed up royally. I had run double wires and made the circuits throughout the church but had not split the wire, so that a single wire was just looped around, returning to the second terminal at the generator creating a direct short circuit. I clipped the wire allowing the AC current to function and had success at last. Father Thomas was so elated that he invited me for lunch every day through Christmas. The meals made Uncle Sam's kitchen a loser. The church had its own cooks and delicious meals.

Father Thomas and I became good friends. They called me, Abraham, reminding me about the Old Testament. In our many conversations over lunch I let it be known that I had artistic talents. Now came my second BIG challenge. Father Thomas took me for a walk down where something like a manger scene appeared. Except you had to use your imagination. Many characters in the manger scene were in very bad condition. Mary's back was broken, the donkey and camel needed hip replacements, little Jesus' color had completely faded and showed chip marks all over. Most importantly, there was no star of Bethlehem.

I went to the PX and purchased plaster, paint, wads of cotton, wood strips, thin paper maché and all the supplies needed for the manger scene. You must remember this nation had been devastated and ruined by the Japanese occupation. After four days of work the

In the Beginning There Was Laughter

manger scene was complete. We installed the speaker system. I want to emphasize that the Japanese POW's contributed a lot in the placement of all the installations.

Christmas came and we had a full house. I remember Bing Crosby singing "I'm Dreaming of a White Christmas" and all the standard Christmas melodies. Everyone seemed happy despite the fact that the church had no organ because the Japanese had removed it. I wrote John Colucci a letter about the whole event and received a care package that lasted me two weeks. In my letter I told him about this GI coming into the church on a heavy workday; everyone was in basic army dress such as a pair of pants and bare chests. The other priests were working somewhere and Father Thomas was at a conference in Manila. This GI comes to me and nervously blabs, "Father, I would like to confess." I told him the confession booth had been destroyed and had not been reconstructed. He said, "Well, I stole my best friend's wallet and lost over $200 in a crap game and I am ashamed of myself." Not having heard a confession before I said to him, "Don't worry, my son, my lips are sealed." I noticed when he left he was scratching his head.

Catholic Church in Batangas, Philippines. Our camp was behind the church.

Abe Kleiman

As mentioned before, we lived in a ten-man tent. We existed under the same weather conditions every day. It was hot, humid and we had a tropical rainstorm almost every day. The most popular person living in our tent was Tommy Dorf from Wisconsin. He was about 24 years of age and his claim to fame was that he was a professional middleweight boxer. He was undefeated in all his fights. The biggest pastime was boxing because it was a live emotional sports event and we had no other real form of entertainment. Remember that all we had for entertainment was a PA system with music records and some short wave radio. We were proud of Tommy because he represented our base of 300 troops. Tommy was friendly and funny. One boring day, Tommy asked me to spar with him to keep him in shape. I said, "NO WAY!" I wanted to live another day. He explained to me that it would be just moving around and just touching and presented me with what he called soft boxing gloves. I told him I was a poor candidate to spar with because I had never had a boxing lesson. He insisted and I said, "What the hell let's box." He tied my gloves on me and I had no other protection, not even a helmet to protect my head. We began to box in the tent, which only had a narrow walking path. Circling around the tent, we had little room: each of us had a sleeping cot with mattress and pillow and a footlocker opposite our bed. All the footlockers were located in the middle of the tent with the beds reaching out toward the end of the tent. So we could only box in that small aisle. All of a sudden lightning struck and I actually froze in one position with my arms up, fists covering my face and before I could count to three I was hit three times and my knees started to buckle and I was falling. Tommy instinctively stopped punching and I instinctively shot out with my left hand with all my strength and hit him square on his chin. Tommy Dorf hit the deck with a thump. I was amazed that I had knocked this man down and he did not move. Now there had just been the two of us boxing and from all over the base people started streaming towards our tent. I thought he was dead. Twenty seconds, no movement. I got down on my hands and knees trying to revive him but my gloves were on.

Someone thought quickly and grabbed a pail of water and spilled it over Tommy's face. Finally Tommy moved and opened his eyes,

In the Beginning There Was Laughter

got up off the ground and said, "OK let's continue." I told him it was over. Tommy was very embarrassed and we stopped sparring. I had a concussion that day but would not let anyone know about it. That night Tommy and the boys planned an evening for me, wining and dining me. When four prostitutes showed up I called it quits. I had remembered seeing training films on venereal diseases and said, "thanks, but no thanks."

Our base functioned well. The landing craft were maintained and repaired as needed. By now almost all the older and experienced vets had sailed for home. If it had not been for the Japanese prisoners whom we kept at our base we could not have completed our duties in repairing and keeping our boats actively running. Now, all the kids were just hanging around. We would line up for "chow" (breakfast, lunch and dinner). Sometimes we would get uninvited guests. Our kitchen supplies and cooks were in tents but we were served outdoors via lineup. We carried our own canteens, (plates, knives, forks and spoons) or we just placed an open can between our hands and served ourselves whatever was in those rectangular trays that were set up with a large spoon in each tray. Just like an open air brunch. You just waited in line for your turn. The uninvited guests were Japanese soldiers roaming the jungles. They became brazen when hungry and just got in line. The young recruits in our outfit could not tell the difference. In our line we had Filipino laborers and Japanese prisoners working at the base waiting in the food line. One day, waiting in line some guy said, "What's that terrible odor?" Looking each other over we noticed this one individual who stunk to high heaven. Yep, it was a Japanese intruder. He gave up meekly as we grabbed him from the line and brought him to headquarters.

The rumors finally came true and I, along with most of the army personnel, received orders to ship out to Hawaii. We packed our duffel bags and were on our way. Leaving the Philippines was a very joyous occasion for me.

Abe Kleiman

How I Fell in Love with Hawaii

    The ship ride to Hawaii was a disaster. The engines broke down in the middle of the Pacific Ocean. On deck as far as the eye could see everyone was doubled over the rail heaving. This situation continued for six days. Seasickness affected everyone on board. Rumor had it that a tidal wave was heading toward Hawaii and we were close to our destination. Everyone was ordered below deck and all the hatches were closed. I could not believe what I heard on the PA system: "everyone pray." No sooner had the announcement been made when the engines started again. It was a miracle that the mess hall became crowded. We had not eaten for six days. The tidal wave never happened and when we landed we boarded busses and I ended up at an Air Force base called Wheeler Field. Yes I ended up in the Air Force and my discharge papers show that I was in the US Army and in the US Army Air Force. Immediately I was doing KP. This meant I had to rise at 4:30 a.m., go to the kitchen and perform manual work for many days. Then one day they ordered me into this hanger and I was told I was to learn about the P51 Mustang. I would be taught to maintain this plane and service the aircraft in this and other hangers on the airfield. Well, this was not my cup of tea and soon became my low period. I did not like what they had planned for me.

    One day I noticed on the bulletin board a request for athletes to try out for the Wheeler Field baseball team. It seems many of the ball players were being discharged. I had loved playing ball back home and had played for my high school team for a short period. I reported for a tryout out of desperation. I did not like being an aircraft mechanic and did not like getting up at 4:30 every morning. I lived in the Bronx, New York, and was a New York Yankee fan and on my questionnaire I stated that I had tried out for the New York Yankees. (I lied.) Now comes the scary part. They gave me a baseball glove, shoes, cap and asked me to go out to the outfield and catch some fly balls. Needless to say, I was nervous but I was also desperate. Then they asked me to get in the batting cage and swing a bat. After a week of practice I went back to my routine and was sure I would not be selected to play on the team, recalling all the other athletes who appeared professional - strong throwing, pitching, batting. How could I make the team? After a rigorous day of KP I pooped out about two

In the Beginning There Was Laughter

p.m. and taking my shoes off with the intent of lying down I noticed an envelope on my bed.

"Private Abraham Kleiman, you have been selected to attend practice starting Wednesday morning and on a regular basis be present at the Wheeler Field baseball stadium at 12 noon at which time you will pick up your baseball uniform and other equipment." Could this be a mistake? Was this a dream? Wheeler Air Force Base was a permanent base. Our barracks were four-story high brick buildings with permanent indoor kitchens and the appearance of a high-class cafeteria and no mud floors. The outside area was beautifully landscaped, better than home, which was five to six story tenement buildings. Now if I understood correctly, I could sleep until 9 a.m., and eat breakfast late. On my way to my first day I questioned myself, *How did I make the team when our Air Force base has so many thousands of personnel around?* I put on my uniform, which was a little tight but I wasn't about to complain. Then I was assigned my locker. I opened the locker and noticed a nameplate that said "Joe DiMaggio." I almost fell off my stool. It seems that during the war Joe DiMaggio had played ball at Wheeler Field. As a kid growing up in the Bronx, Joe DiMaggio had been my hero, my idol. What a thrill!

Now it is down to business. I am playing in the outfield, left field to be exact, and it is 85 degrees Fahrenheit. I remove my shirt since it is a practice session. The next day they have a practice game and I am very nervous. I think they might find out I never tried out with the New York Yankees. Circumstances are that a batter has reached third base. All I can remember is a line drive out in front of me and I frantically ran in, dive and make a shoestring catch doing a somersault. I leap to my feet, the runner at third tags up and races toward home plate and with follow through motion I throw the ball with all my energy. The ball is a perfect strike and the runner is 20 feet from home plate. Is anyone watching? Hey, that was the best play of my life! Hello? Did anyone see that play?! I look into the dugout. No one is moving. After the third out I come trotting in and no one says anything. The next morning I am at the field. The manager, approaches me and says, "Hey lefty, go out to the mound and pitch." Ball in hand, I walk out toward the pitching mound as if I am in a western film. However, I am thinking, *Will I survive?* Trying to keep my demeanor, I approach the mound. Here I am, a 19-year-old kid who with some bullshit got to play baseball with a group of very talented ball players from double- and triple-A baseball leagues. Now, I had never pitched in a baseball game before and I had never been coached or had instruction. So, I focus my thoughts on some major league pitchers. In the Philippines I remember watching an American League pitcher named Gordon Maltzburger or some such name. I thought back to watching the New York Yankees' Lefty Gomez and others. The guy I am pitching to is about six foot two, muscular and mean looking. I get in about twelve practice pitches before this batter comes to the plate but I am not loose. So I rear back and throw my first pitch and hear a grunt. When I look at the plate, there is the batter sprawled face down over it. I assume the pitch was right at him and he has reacted in fear of being hit. I hear the umpire yell, "Ball," and his left finger goes up in the air. The batter brushes the dirt off his uniform and sets his legs at the plate but he does not look mean. I sense a look of fear. Now I am thinking, *Throw the ball like the time you threw out the runner from third base.* "Strike," I hear, then, "Strike," again. I have him. One ball, two strikes, now I have my confidence. The next pitch, I hear this cracking noise and the ball goes into right field like a bullet. A base hit. There goes my confidence. The next batter is a right-handed hitter but small, about five foot eight. He looks nervous. First pitch in the dirt but he swings at it. Now my confidence returns. I try this pitch where my knuckle goes behind the ball and my pinkie and forefinger and thumb are around the ball. It's a fast overhand motion but the ball moves slowly to the plate. I must have seen this pitch in the movies. He swings at my motion and I have him 0 and 2. The next pitch is low, he doesn't swing. Then over the plate, line drive right at me. I put my glove up to my face for protection, the ball goes into my glove and I throw to first, a double play. I do not recall anyone scoring on me that inning.

The interesting thing was after my first pitching experience the pitching coach started working with me on my pitching. My hitting improved over time and overall I stayed on the team but did not become a regular player. That was OK with me because throughout my stay in Hawaii I slept until 8 a.m. every day and was at the field by 11a.m. for practice. Then we traveled to other bases on other islands in Hawaii. After each game we received a gourmet meal at the mess halls we visited. Overall it was a great experience. Then the

In the Beginning There Was Laughter

baseball season ended and I went into a panic. Do I have to go back to KP and early wake-up again? Then on the bulletin board an announcement jumped out at me. "Attention, any athletes with football experience, present yourself at the field for tryouts at 12 noon." Here we go again.

    About fifty applicants show up. Now with new protective gear on, I present myself to a coach who promptly requests that I get in line with six other guys. I am instructed to run ten yards, cut left and a pass will be thrown at me. To my surprise I catch the pass. Then I have to play scrimmage. I am to receive the ball from a center and run through in a football formation then run through the opposition in a scrimmage and these guys are coming at me to tackle me and I am hit from two sides and down I go. I must have six hundred pounds on top of me. So I am in great pain. This goes on for two weeks and I decide to surrender. I am five foot nine weighing 165 pounds. Mathematically I am overmatched. Most of the guys are over six foot, built like trucks and weighing well over two hundred pounds. My goal, though, had been not to go back to Army life and getting up at 4:30 a.m. The next morning I receive my orders. I am going home. The timing could not have been more perfect.

Abe Kleiman

Happy NOT to be on KP duty at 4:30 am. Circa 1945 at Wheeler Air Base, Oahu, Hawaii.

Royal Hawaiian Resort Hotel, Oahu, Hawaii. The good old days. Notice no high rises, hotels or condos.

Lounging on a catamaran, Waikiki beach, Oahu Hawaii. The best vacation.

In the Beginning There Was Laughter

Wheeler Field Air Force Base was paradise. Permanent brick and concrete. Built better than my apartment house in the Bronx.

Abe Kleiman

Hanging around Wheeler Airfield.

In the Beginning There Was Laughter

Home at Last!

The GI bill was the best thing that could have happened to me and I used it to its maximum, completing college and art school. However, my army life had been strange and, as I experienced it, very comical. I guarded prisoners of war from Germany and Japan. I played baseball with future baseball pros including Clint Hartling, the Hondo Hurricane, who was under contract with the New York Giants, I knocked out a professional boxer and many other strange experiences. One of my most lasting memorable events happened later in life. Around 1975 I still enjoyed playing softball. We had a local softball league, which I played with occasionally.

In one game our team in its beautiful uniforms reaches a critical time. This is a must-win game in order to make the playoffs. The telephone rings'; it's the manager asking me if I can rush down to the ball field to bat. When I get down to the field in less than three minutes wearing my Sunday work-around-the-house outfit I am rushed to the plate. Our team is down by one run we have two outs and it is the last inning with one man on base. It certainly is a tense moment. All I can remember is the sound of making contact with the ball, driving it well over the right fielder's head. It is a great thrill running the bases and hearing the roar from the crowd. However, my legs will not cooperate as I chug past second base. I notice the outfielder retrieving the ball; my speed diminishes quickly and as I round third I am stumbling toward home and the team is encouraging me to speed up. Now I really had not prepared for this event. My pockets jingle with loose change and a set of about eight keys for the house and our two cars. Lou Agnesini, our team's first baseman and resident executive in charge of finance for the team joins in yelling, "Slide!" After the dust clears at home plate I notice the umpire yelling, "Safe!" and a tumultuous roar going up. Then I rise to my feet brushing off all the dirt. I notice my trousers were shredded in the slide, my keys in my pocket have cut into my skin, and I am bleeding. At that moment Lou says, "You won the game, now give me two dollars!" It seems anyone playing ball must contribute two dollars per game for equipment and insurance. That was my last game.

Street Wise

Growing up in the Bronx meant you had to have a survival instinct. For example: On our block we hung around with different groups that we liked to be with which were basically the guys I went to school with. In my situation and time, these were junior high students and no girls. We played stickball, touch football, and softball. A group of guys on our block challenged us to a football game. We accepted this challenge on a Sunday morning at Trojan Field in the Bronx. We were excited about the game and after walking three miles to the field we found a football field that was vacant. Trojan field was a large complex of eight fields and loosely arranged and did not have line markers. Our method was to walk off the distance gained or lost. The game started. I was a lineman and I was about four foot eight at the time. Our team won the toss of the coin. After a long huddle we had our plays planned. We lined up for our first play. We had no equipment like shoulder pads and no uniforms. All we had was a deep spirit. Our team was made up of average 14-year-olds. Our opponents' average age was 16 to 17 years.

When we line up for the first play the ball is snapped back to our quarterback, Frank, and like lightning Frank is on the ground with three tacklers on top of him. This time we go into a huddle with fear in our hearts. Frank says, "I sprained my ankle and can't play." He limps off the field. We have fifteen guys and after the first play the guys on the sidelines do not look too anxious to play. (It was common practice to ask anybody on the sidelines to play because most of the games were "pickup" games. There were lots of guys who wanted to be quarterbacks and win that big game to become instant heroes.) We get our replacement, some guy named Jim. As we line up for the next play I am on the line in front of Leo who is 17, five foot two, about 170 pounds, built like a tank. My size, as I said, is four foot eight and weighing in at 120 pounds. The tallest guy on their team is five foot seven and weighs in at 180 pounds. Our biggest guy is five foot three and 140 pounds. The math comes late to us but, remember, our team will not give up. We will not cave in to these beasts. The ball is snapped and Leo, the lineman, comes at me like a bull. I stand aside like a toreador with a cape. Needless to say, in four plays we lost fifteen yards and the bleeding quarterback left the game. That afternoon we lost five quarterbacks, but to our credit as a team we did not forfeit the game or our dignity.

Jacob's Corner

In my family, as I am sure in other families, we have one or two individuals who somehow seem to create or present humor. I have a grandson named Jacob. He is bright and has a good command of the English language. However, he is always thinking about things that turn into very humorous situations. Although I have forgotten most of them, I have recorded others such as the following:

While riding in a car with my wife and daughter, Jacob asks Grandma, "Do you know what I'm thinking about? Most older men seem to go to the bathroom a lot and our president is an older man. When he stands up in front of an audience to make a speech, which can last an hour or two, and he gets the urge, they should build a urinal into the stand that he is speaking from and he can use it when needed. No one would know." "That stand is called a podium," says his Mom. "We could call it a peedium," says Jacob.

One day at 11 a.m. I observe my seven-year-old grandson eating a bowl of dry cereal. What strikes me most is the speed with which he is eating. I promptly call to him and ask, "Jacob, what is your hurry. Are you late? Do you have to be someplace?" He says no and proceeds to eat quickly and I ask him, "Why are you still eating so quickly?" His response is, "You don't understand, Poppy. It is after 11a.m. and I have to finish eating before 12 noon. That's when it is lunchtime."

Abe Kleiman

When the news broke about Monica Lewinksy and President Clinton it was splashed over every TV station and, needless to say, it reached my grandson's ears. His comment was, "I can't understand why Monica Lewinsky got into so much trouble. Why couldn't she keep her mouth shut?"

One of the enjoyments of my retirement is watching my grandchildren playing in Little League. Here I am watching my grandson and his team waging war with the opposition in a Little League with all the equipment you see in the Major Leagues. We are the Cardinals and we are losing by six runs. In their last at bat the Cardinals come from behind in heroic fashion and with great excitement and fanfare win the ball game. This ecstatic grandfather rushes over to his ten-year-old grandson and, jokester that I am, I requests his autograph. Spontaneously his immediate response is, "Sorry, no solicitations please."

In the Beginning There Was Laughter

MY EARLY PERIOD

Abe Kleiman

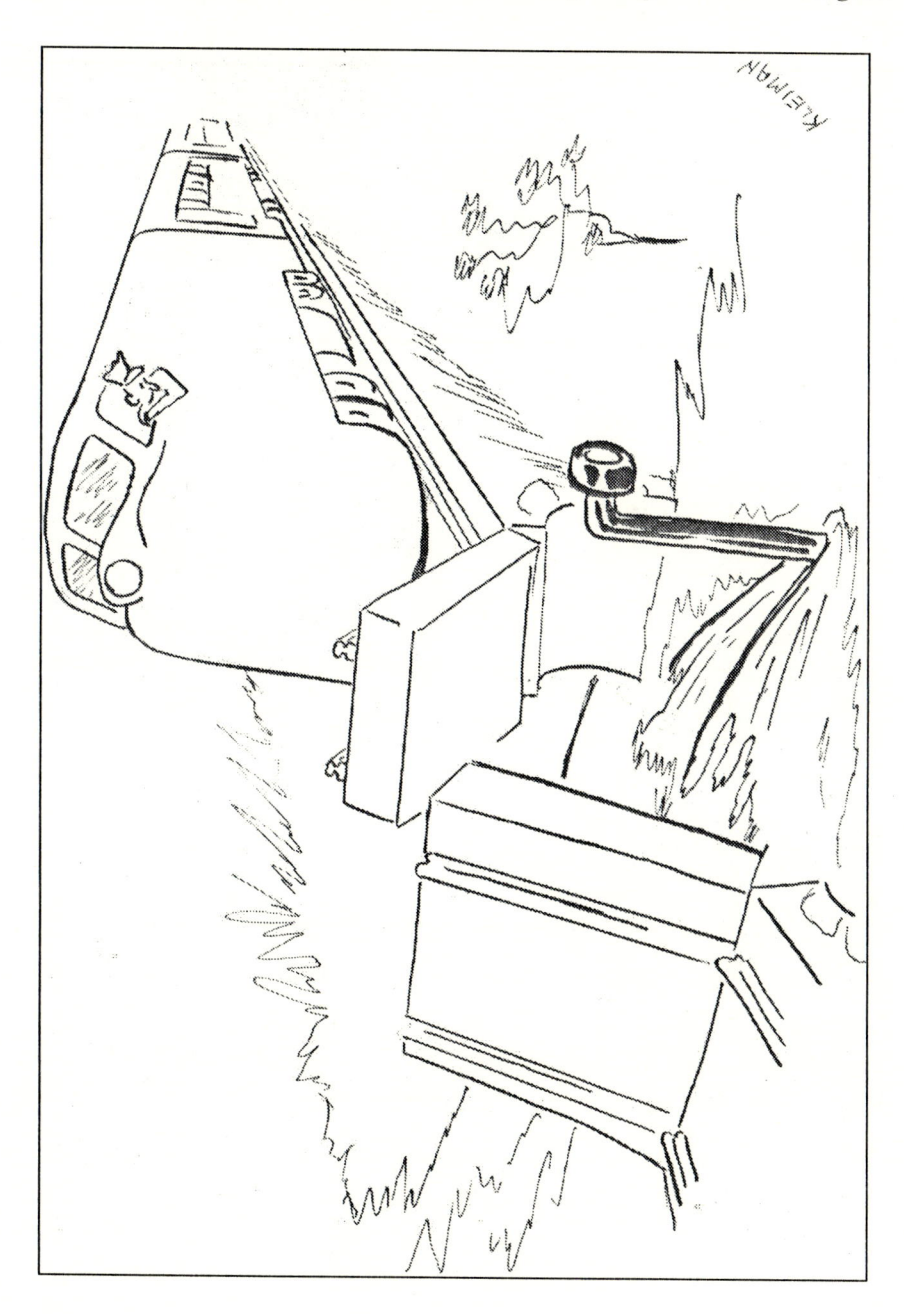

In the Beginning There Was Laughter

Abe Kleiman

"This ought to make you melt, Mr. Hinkle. You are the father of triplets!"

In the Beginning There Was Laughter

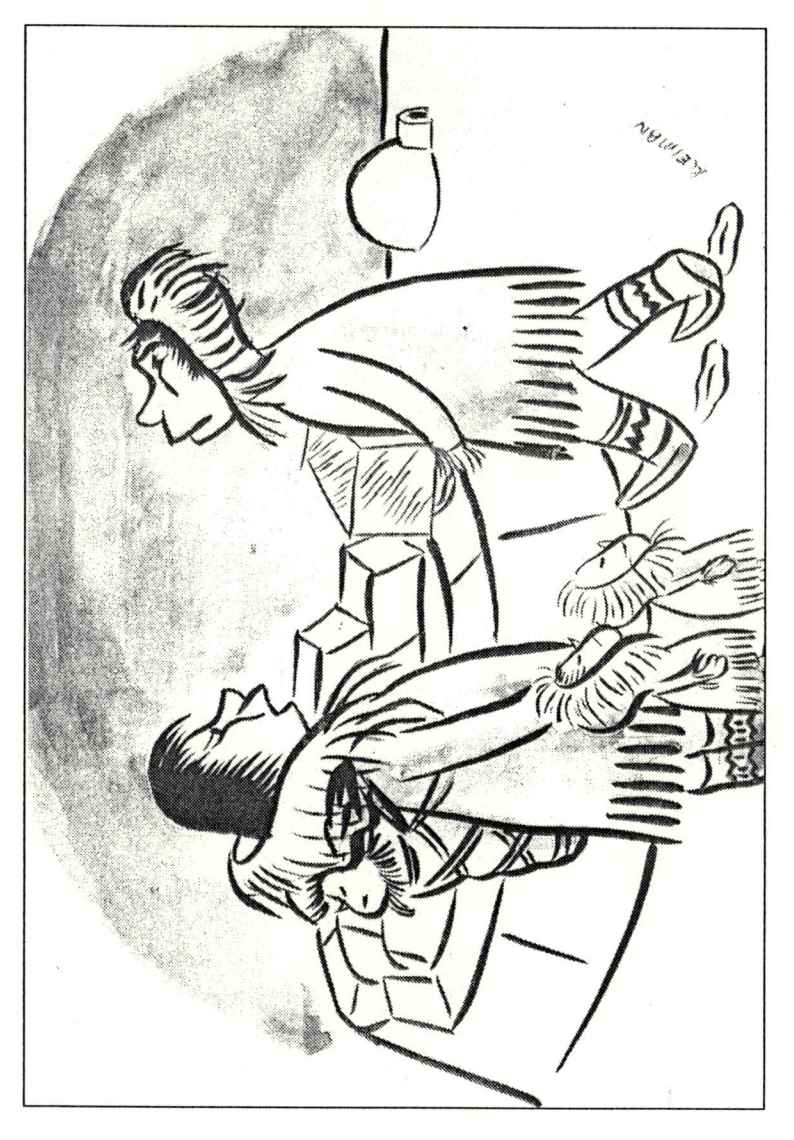

"Don't forget to leave a hole on top for the television antenna!"

Abe Kleiman

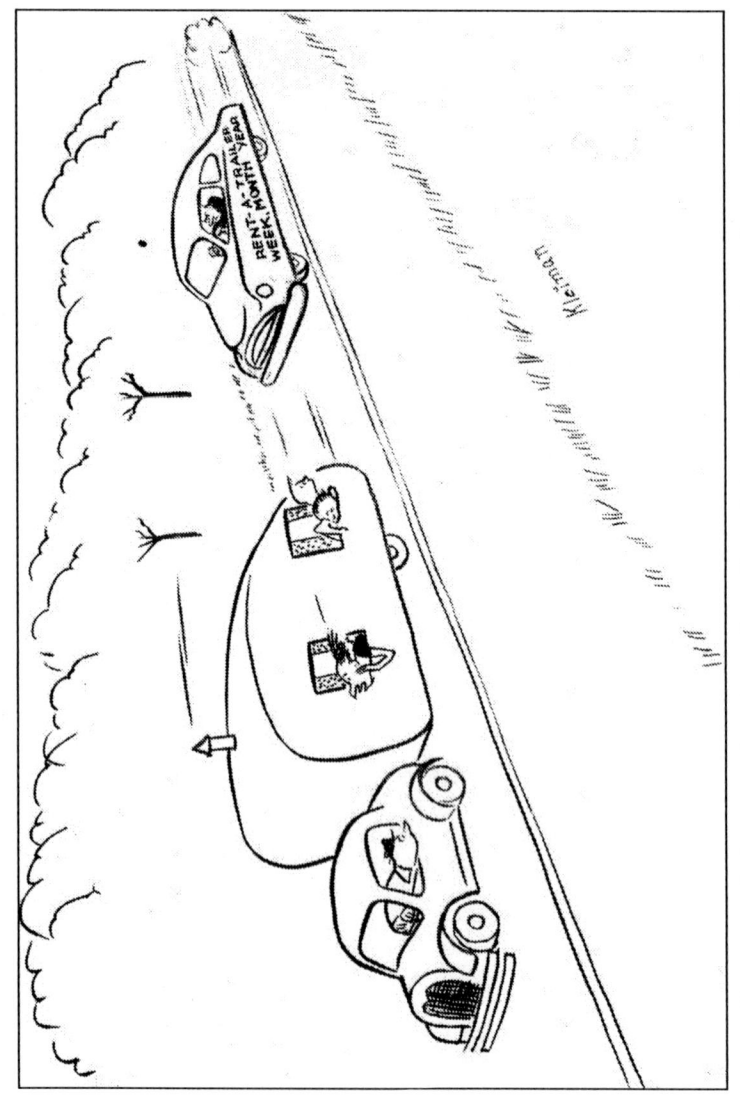

"Faster! Faster! The landlord is coming for the rent!"

In the Beginning There Was Laughter

Abe Kleiman

In the Beginning There Was Laughter

Abe Kleiman

"It's a gift certificate at McDonalds!"

In the Beginning There Was Laughter

"You win lady! Your demonstration beats mine!"

Abe Kleiman

"Cathy! Turn me over and rub me on the other side!"

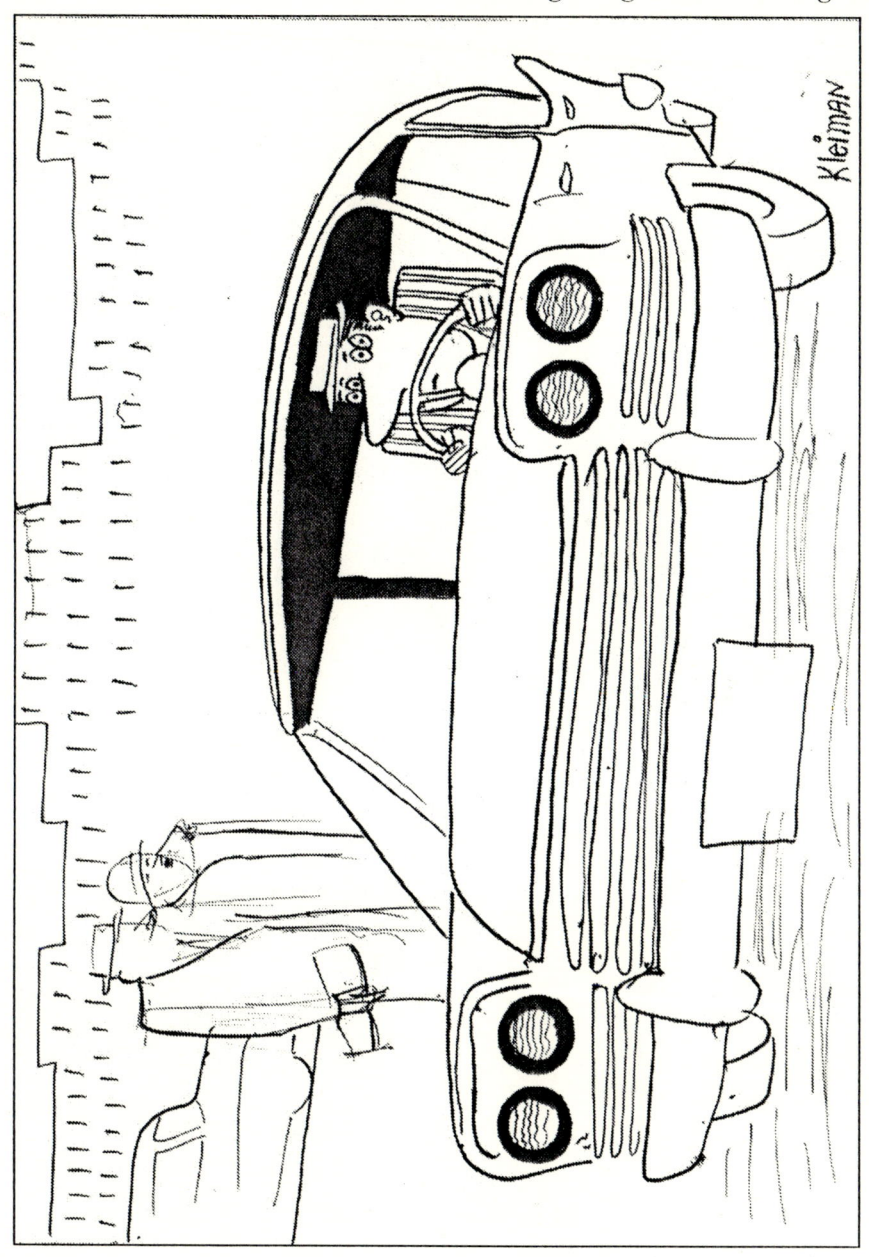

In the Beginning There Was Laughter

Abe Kleiman

"Drucker coming in to pinch-hit for Klinski and Sidewell to help Drucker hold the bat!"

In the Beginning There Was Laughter

"Why just the other day they spotted a submarine only three miles off shore!"

Abe Kleiman

"He is in the clean up battallion"

In the Beginning There Was Laughter

Abe Kleiman

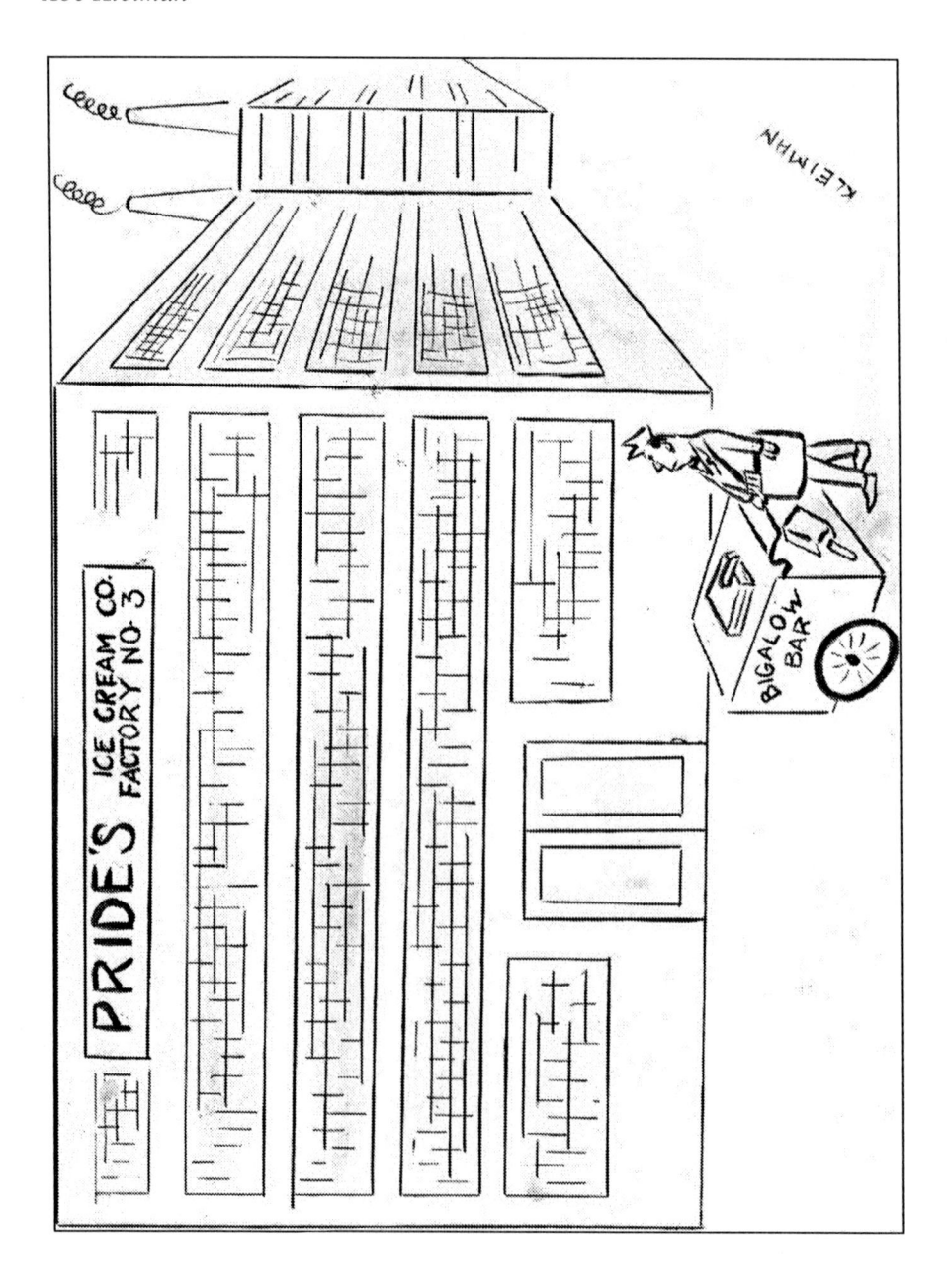

In the Beginning There Was Laughter

"Yes you can come down for a drink of water, but not this way!"

Abe Kleiman

"They say after 20 years
married couples begin to look alike!"

In the Beginning There Was Laughter

"Odd looking fellow."

Abe Kleiman

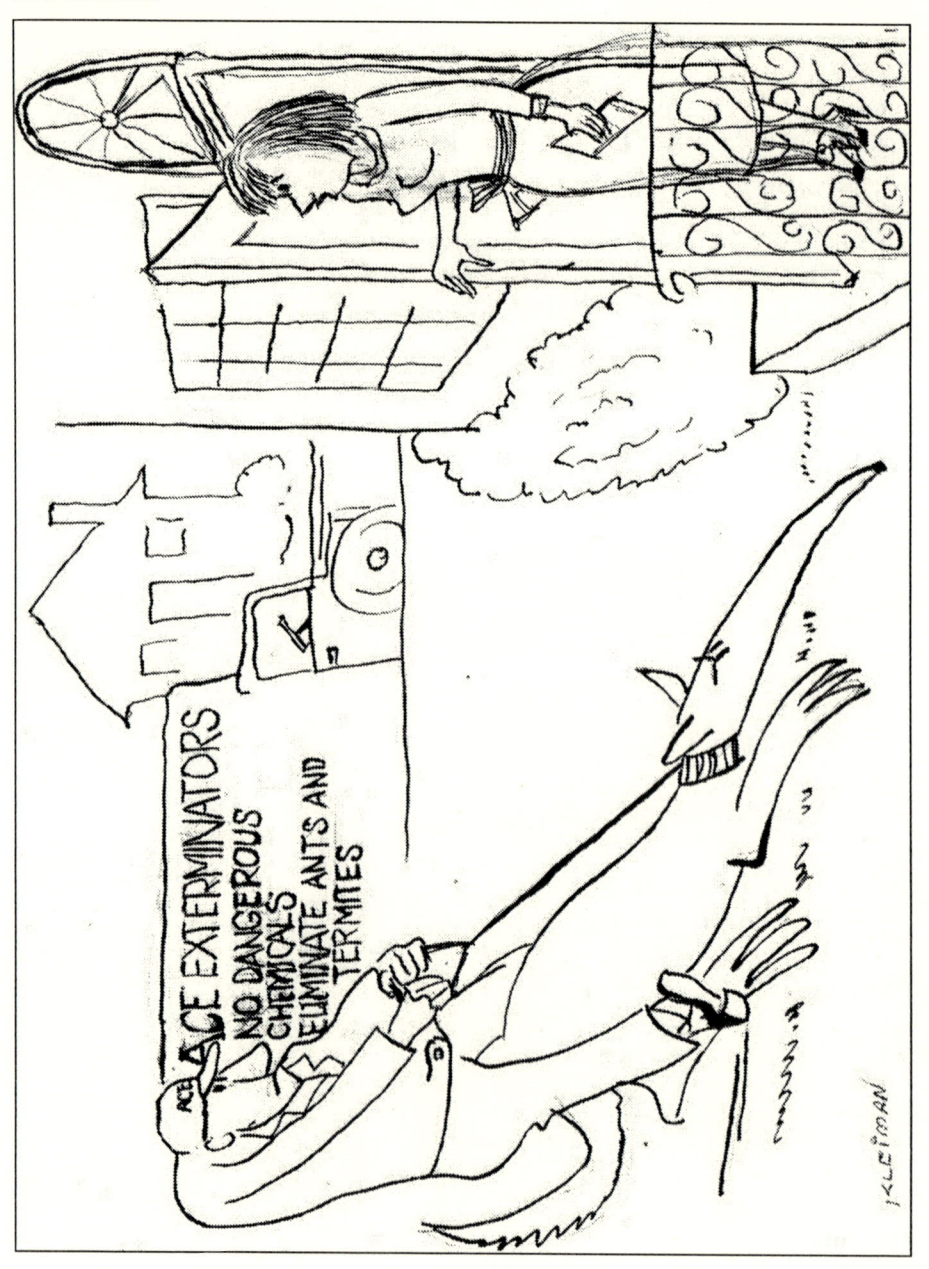

In the Beginning There Was Laughter

"Where is that little runt we call a dishwasher?"

Abe Kleiman

"Sorry I'm late boss, but some creep ran in front of my car!"

In the Beginning There Was Laughter

"Two containers of coffee please,
one without sugar!"

Abe Kleiman

"Ah! I see that you are from Missouri."

In the Beginning There Was Laughter

"No, I'm not working overtime.
I dropped my car key!"

Abe Kleiman

"Sorry son, but where I come from we don't drink water."

In the Beginning There Was Laughter

Abe Kleiman

"When are you going to let your daughter stand on her own two feet?"

In the Beginning There Was Laughter

"Have you seen a love sick couple around?"

Abe Kleiman

"Somehow H.G. I don't think your mind has been on your work."

In the Beginning There Was Laughter

"I told you the coffee was strong!"

Abe Kleiman

"I'm a size twelve all right.
Look at how loose it is!"

In the Beginning There Was Laughter

Abe Kleiman

"Throw the doll at me, break my glasses! Wait 'til we get home!"

In the Beginning There Was Laughter

"XI XII XIII XIV XV"

Abe Kleiman

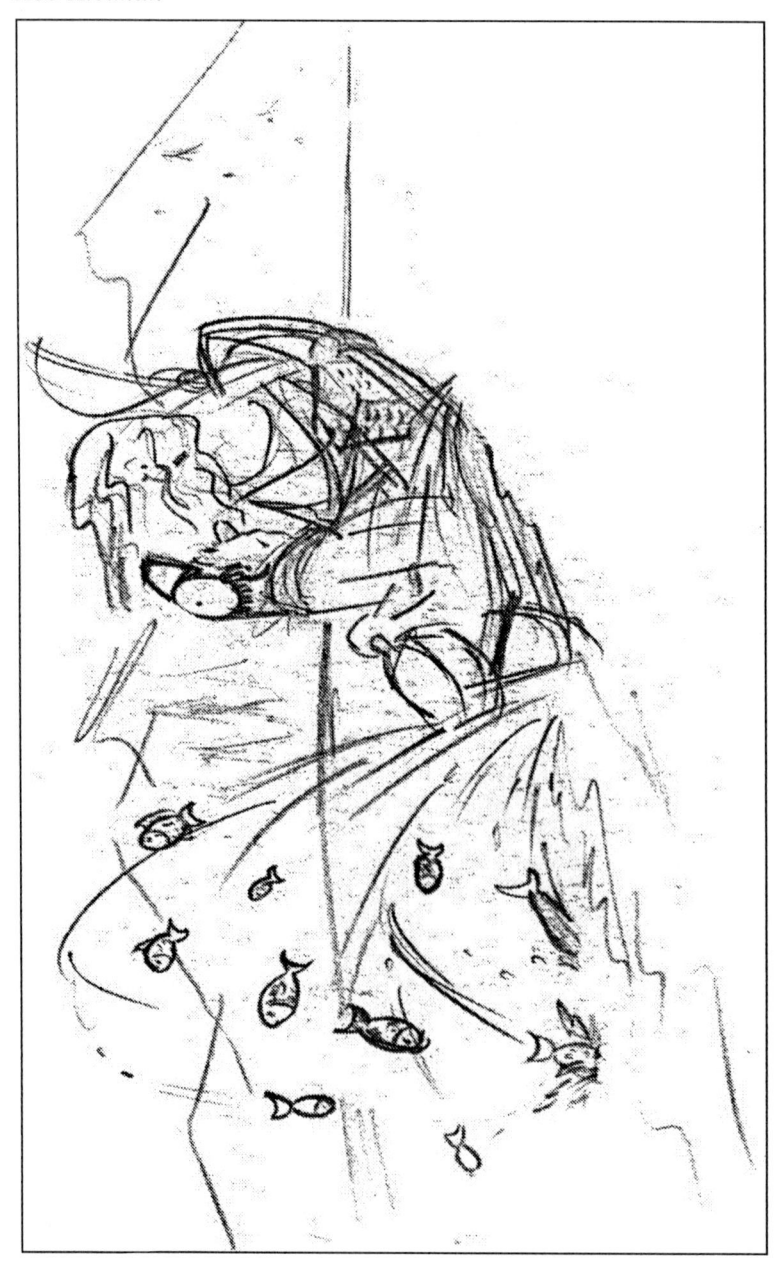

"Stop here! I've got a hunch this is a good spot!"

In the Beginning There Was Laughter

"Where can I get some acid, which doesn't eat through paper, but when touched by human hands..."

Abe Kleiman

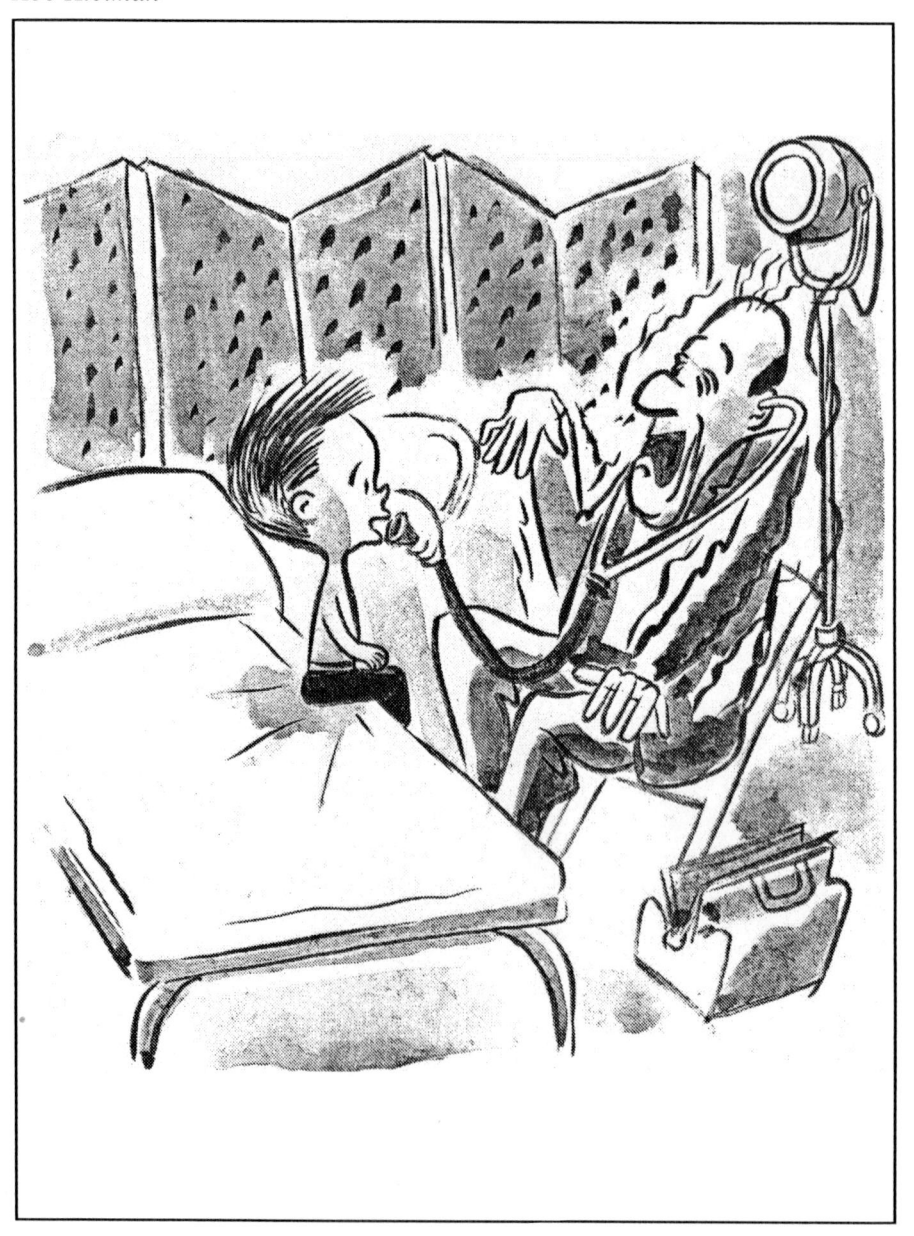

"Space Station One, do you read me?!"

In the Beginning There Was Laughter

Abe Kleiman

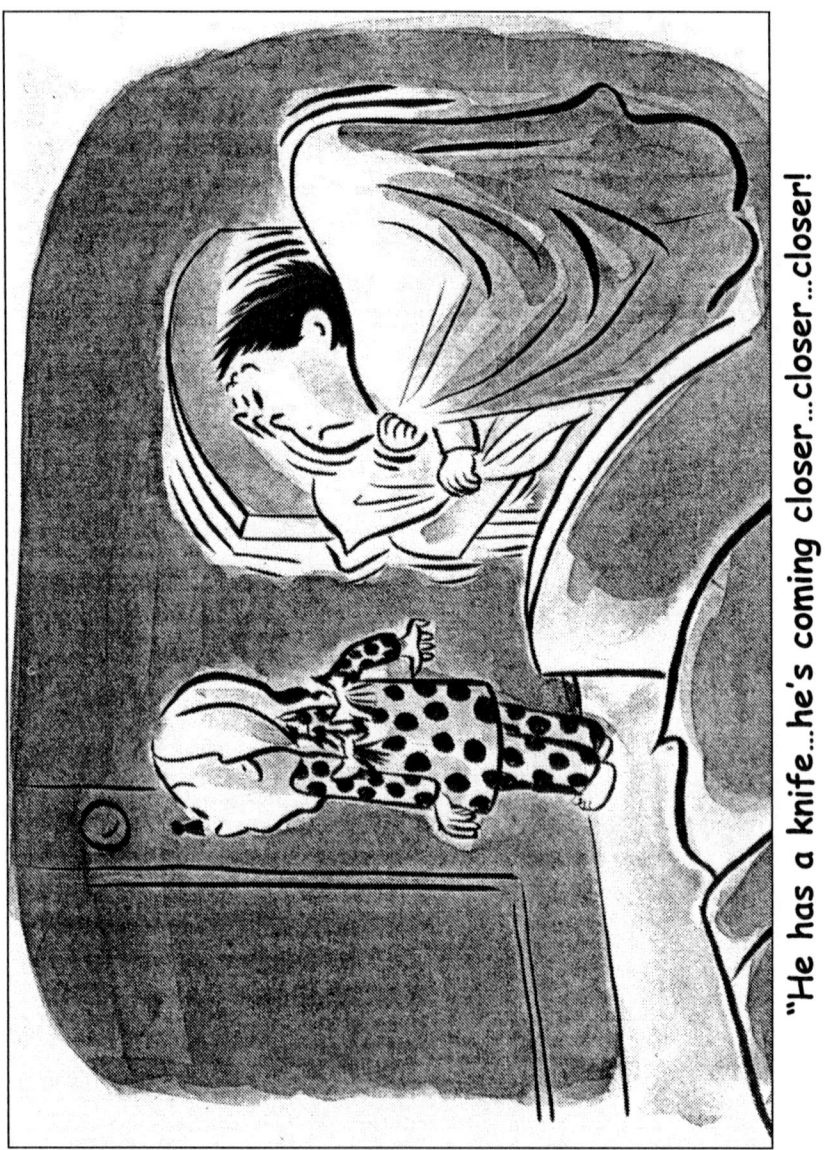

"He has a knife...he's coming closer...closer...closer! Gee Whiz, Ma just turned off the television!"

In the Beginning There Was Laughter

Abe Kleiman

"That's a husband for you. All evening he wants to go home but when it comes time to leave, he can't be found!"

In the Beginning There Was Laughter

"Have you any
"Drop Dead" greeting cards?"

Abe Kleiman

In the Beginning There Was Laughter

"They are really biting today. Pop!"

Abe Kleiman

"You're going to stick your head out that window once too often!"

In the Beginning There Was Laughter

"I wish that you would stop putting your name all over the wall!"

Abe Kleiman

"Krumm's Basement! Fish Pets...Fish foods...FISH!!!"

In the Beginning There Was Laughter

"If there be anyone here who objects to this marriage let him speak now..."

Abe Kleiman

"All that music from your
pretty little hands."

In the Beginning There Was Laughter

"This bra's defense broke down before I did."

Abe Kleiman

"Darling, tell me why you love me, in twenty five words or less."

In the Beginning There Was Laughter

"A little bear sleeps in his little bear skin. He is very warm I am told.

Last night I slept in my little bare skin and I caught a heck of a cold."

Abe Kleiman

"Well, didn't you tell me to put a white line down the middle of the street?"

In the Beginning There Was Laughter

Abe Kleiman

"I made it extra firm."

In the Beginning There Was Laughter

"No, but we do have Green Cross and Green Sheild cards!"

Abe Kleiman

"Stop calling it our child;
it's originally Macy's"

In the Beginning There Was Laughter

Abe Kleiman

In the Beginning There Was Laughter

"NO, it's not his hobby...he's had some bad experiences in the bath tub."

Abe Kleiman

"Can't you see how congested these small foreign cars are?"

In the Beginning There Was Laughter

"And where do you think you're going without paying!"

Abe Kleiman

"Now remember comrade, the problem of reentry is in your hands!"

In the Beginning There Was Laughter

Abe Kleiman

"That's the end of our bottleneck!"

In the Beginning There Was Laughter

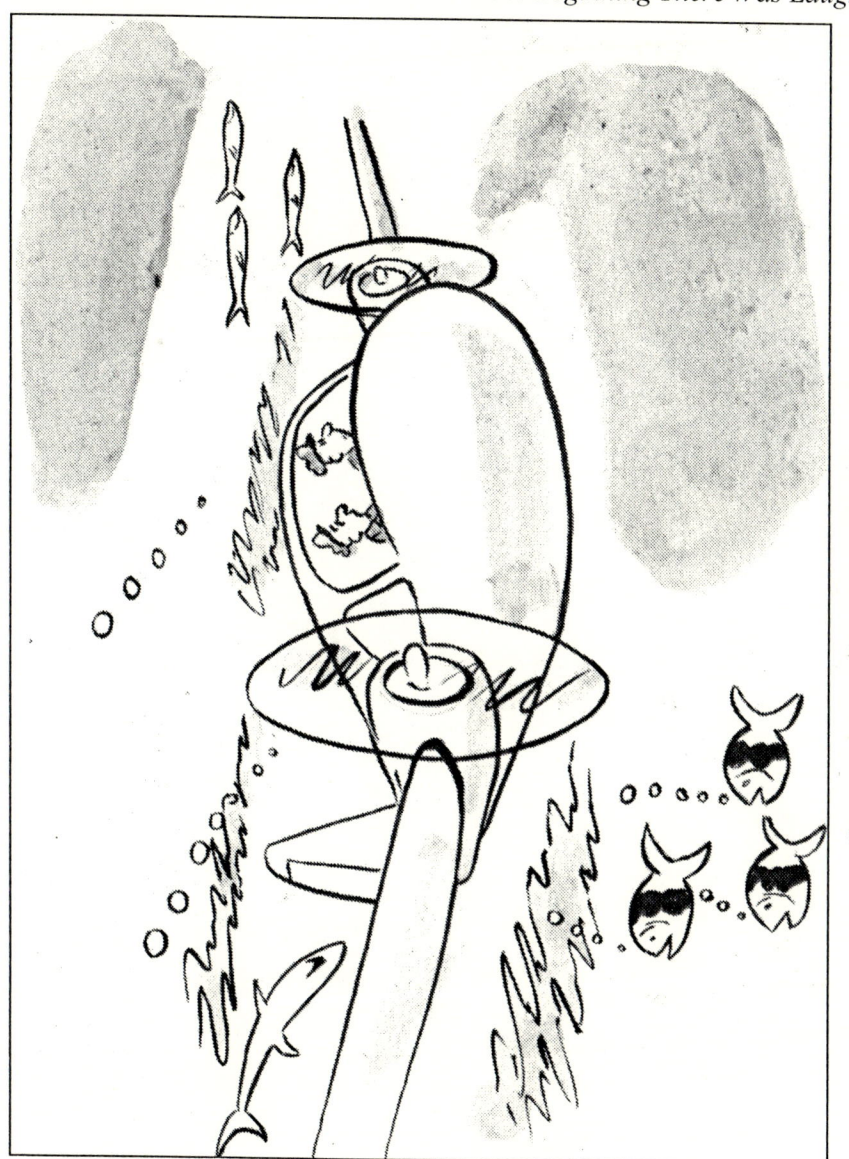

"Some soup! Hey Charley?"

Abe Kleiman

"You and your low low foreign car!"

In the Beginning There Was Laughter

"Miss Latuse! Would you confirm or deny that you sleep in the nude?"

Abe Kleiman

"Did I order all that?"

In the Beginning There Was Laughter

"How could she go to sleep at a time like this?"

109

Abe Kleiman

"Help! I'm all plugged in!"

In the Beginning There Was Laughter

"Pardon my dog Madam, but he still has that maternal instinct!"

Abe Kleiman

"Don't mind me Mr. Smedlow, I'm just the plumber cleaning up after a day's work!"

In the Beginning There Was Laughter

"He just loses himself in his work!"

Abe Kleiman

"Your honor! Could you restrain the witness from staring at the jury!"

In the Beginning There Was Laughter

"For another fifteen cents he can have pie with his coffee!"

Abe Kleiman

MY SPORTS PERIOD

In the Beginning There Was Laughter

"He has his own way of scoring."

117

Abe Kleiman

"This is the nearest thing to
a caddy cart I could find."

In the Beginning There Was Laughter

"Been drinking again, eh Koslowski?"

Abe Kleiman

"Tell me that was not a fair catch!"

In the Beginning There Was Laughter

"Now I know where to begin.
THIS IS A FOOTBALL!"

Abe Kleiman

"If he is out cough once!
If he's safe cough twice!"

In the Beginning There Was Laughter

"He blew on my glasses causing them to fog!"

Abe Kleiman

"I've got a hunch he might try and sneak home."

In the Beginning There Was Laughter

"Who is the wise guy with the magnifying glass?"

Abe Kleiman

"If you don't mind, you are
blocking my view of the ball game."

In the Beginning There Was Laughter

"Forgot to touch third."

Abe Kleiman

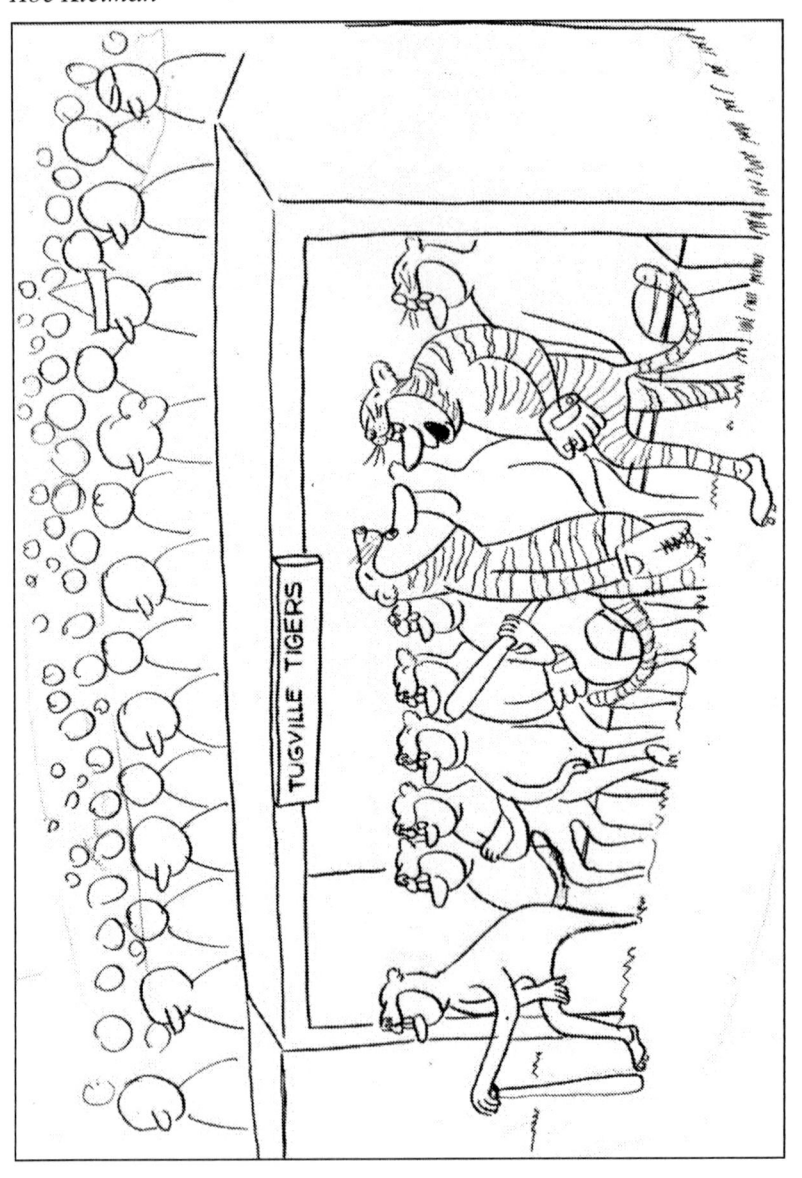

"Don't you think our publicity agent is going to far?"

In the Beginning There Was Laughter

"It's amazing how many accurate decisions you have made, but sometimes..."

Abe Kleiman

"I think it should have been scored a hit."

In the Beginning There Was Laughter

"You've been pitching em low and into the dirt!"

Abe Kleiman

In the Beginning There Was Laughter

"It's starting to drizzle---- it's raining---- the game is held up---- now it's pouring---- you won't believe this folks but—gurgle—gurgle--"

Abe Kleiman

"Is the best dressed ball player in the majors going to set the style with a crease in the front?!"

In the Beginning There Was Laughter

"Come on baby, another fast one!"

Abe Kleiman

"Legal or illegal, he is getting them to hustle."

In the Beginning There Was Laughter

"Can't you see he's trying to bean me?"

Abe Kleiman

"By walking a batter,
I mean pitch four wide ones!"

In the Beginning There Was Laughter

"All I ask is to stop and let me explain how he was safe."

Abe Kleiman

"I'm upper tier,
section 42, row A seat 12."

… *In the Beginning There Was Laughter*

MY LATE PERIOD

Abe Kleiman

In the Beginning There Was Laughter

"His name is Gillette, from the shaving people."

Abe Kleiman

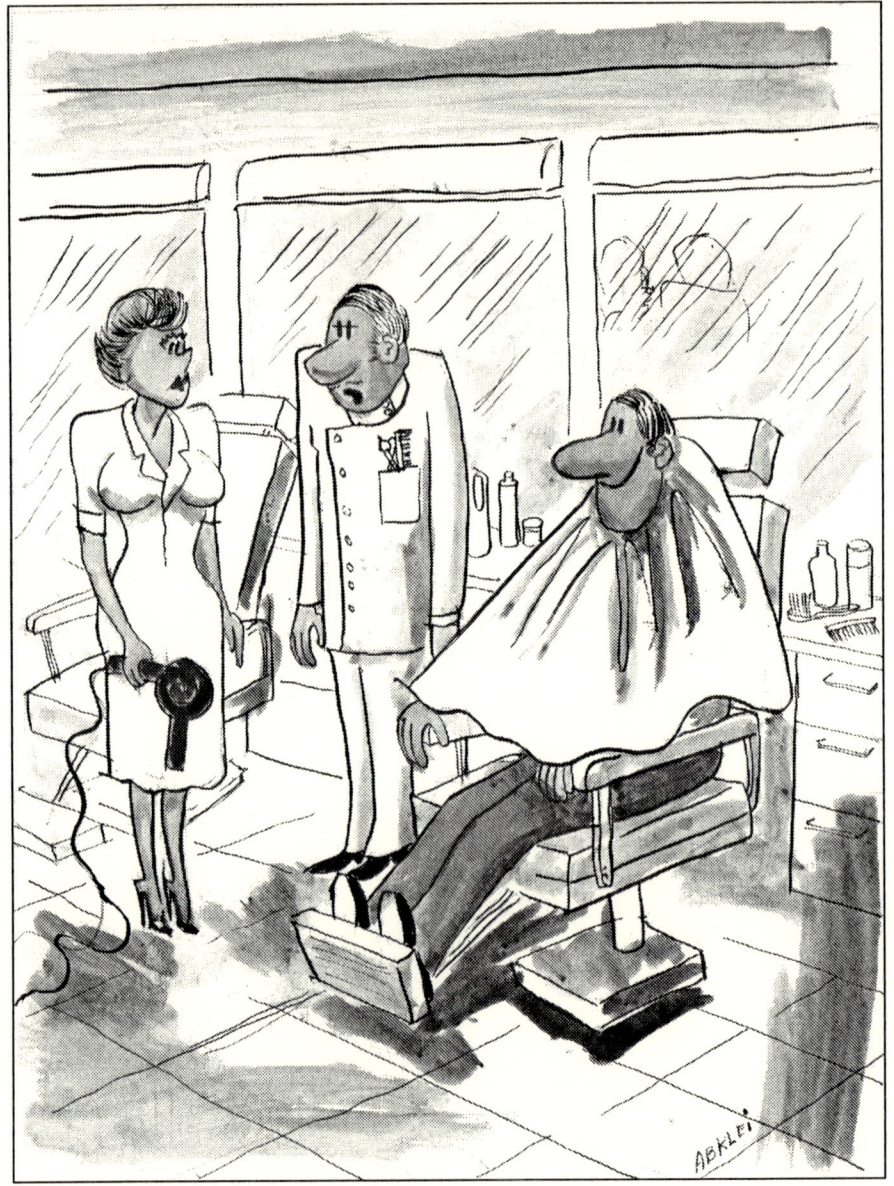

"Max wants a blow job."

In the Beginning There Was Laughter

Invented by Jacob C. Bloom
THE PEEDIUM
This will replace the podium for politicians
Who take longer to complete their speeches!

Abe Kleiman

"My understanding was, he died after taking Viagra."

In the Beginning There Was Laughter

"She suffers from low self esteem."

Abe Kleiman

"Donald never refuses to go see a concert, even though he hates classical music."

In the Beginning There Was Laughter

"They are inseparable."

Abe Kleiman

"All I heard was a lound WSHHHH!"

In the Beginning There Was Laughter

"Front desk! What happened to that magnificent mountain view you promised me?"

Abe Kleiman

"Elizabeth, did I have a close call today!"

In the Beginning There Was Laughter

"Do you give senior citizen discounts?"

Abe Kleiman

"George the soup of the day is
Cream of Asaparagus."

In the Beginning There Was Laughter

"Since this is a "no frills" airline, let me offer a cup of coffee to a hardworking flight attendant."

Abe Kleiman

"The only thing that I can suggest is to change your seating to cargo!"

In the Beginning There Was Laughter

Abe Kleiman

"This toilet is occupied!"

In the Beginning There Was Laughter

Abe Kleiman

"What happened to Harvey? He was fixing our drainage problem!"

In the Beginning There Was Laughter

"How bearish am I? I advise those investors with lots of cash to buy a king size mattress with a zipper on the side, distribute the cash evenly so that you do not get any lumps and then you can sleep soundly."

Abe Kleiman

In the Beginning There Was Laughter

"Yes, Abdulla, I do believe in martyrdom, but I think they are running out of virgins!"

Abe Kleiman

"I'll go with the Paula Jones nose."

In the Beginning There Was Laughter

"Oh Mighty Sultan, your VIAGRA pills have arrived."

Abe Kleiman

In the Beginning There Was Laughter

"But really, I did not inhale."

Abe Kleiman

In the Beginning There Was Laughter

Enterprising new ideas for the new economy.

Abe Kleiman

"Now with this baby, you can forget about miles per gallon."

In the Beginning There Was Laughter

"You see, Howard is doing his part for the foot and mouth disease epidemic."

Abe Kleiman

"We, the Taliban, would like to align ourselves in the war against terrorism."

In the Beginning There Was Laughter

You win some, you lose some

Abe Kleiman

In the Beginning There Was Laughter

"My son-in-law is out of a job. He spent 15 years with the opera "Aida" and it was very highly specialized work and he had to follow the elephants with a shovel, picking up after them. Then they discovered KAOPECTATE."

Abe Kleiman

"Where did you learn about headaches?"

In the Beginning There Was Laughter

"The seventy five cents
I paid was no illusion!"

Abe Kleiman

"I think that I will never see a tree like this where I can pee."

In the Beginning There Was Laughter

"What do you mean I am not allowed on this beach, I am an endangered species!"

Abe Kleiman

"He doesn't own it, he rents it."

In the Beginning There Was Laughter

"Sometimes passion becomes overwhelming, but on the practical side, did I mention the wife and two kids?"

Abe Kleiman

In the Beginning There Was Laughter

"As your tour guide, let me inform you again, the tour is over."

Abe Kleiman

"I'd die for an eggplant lobster roulade over linguini."

In the Beginning There Was Laughter

"We are sorry for the inconvenience. As a valued customer we appreciate your patience. The estimated wait time is fourteen hours and twelve minutes."

Abe Kleiman

"This is the new stamp commemorating the prostitute. It's only twenty cents! However if you lick it it's a dallar."

In the Beginning There Was Laughter

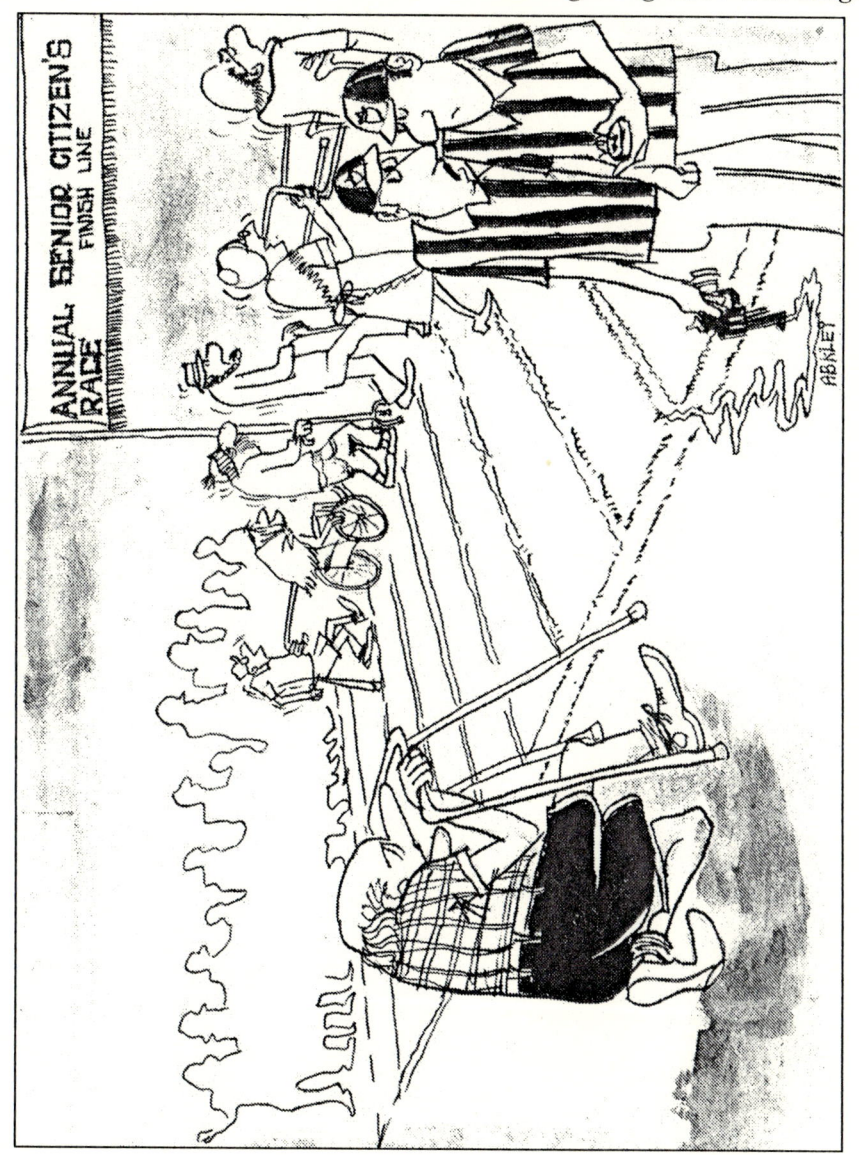

"I think Max forgot his hearing aid!"

Abe Kleiman

"I promised you an erection,
now you have twenty minutes to use it."

In the Beginning There Was Laughter

"I used Rogaine and Viagra."

Abe Kleiman

"Indian Giver!"

In the Beginning There Was Laughter

"How did you know I live in that house on the top of the hill?"

Abe Kleiman

In the Beginning There Was Laughter

"George, I think that this loyalty thing is going too far!"

Abe Kleiman

"I'm having a slow day, sell 200 shares of Microsoft and wire it to my checking account"

In the Beginning There Was Laughter

"That's where he gets his best reception."

Abe Kleiman

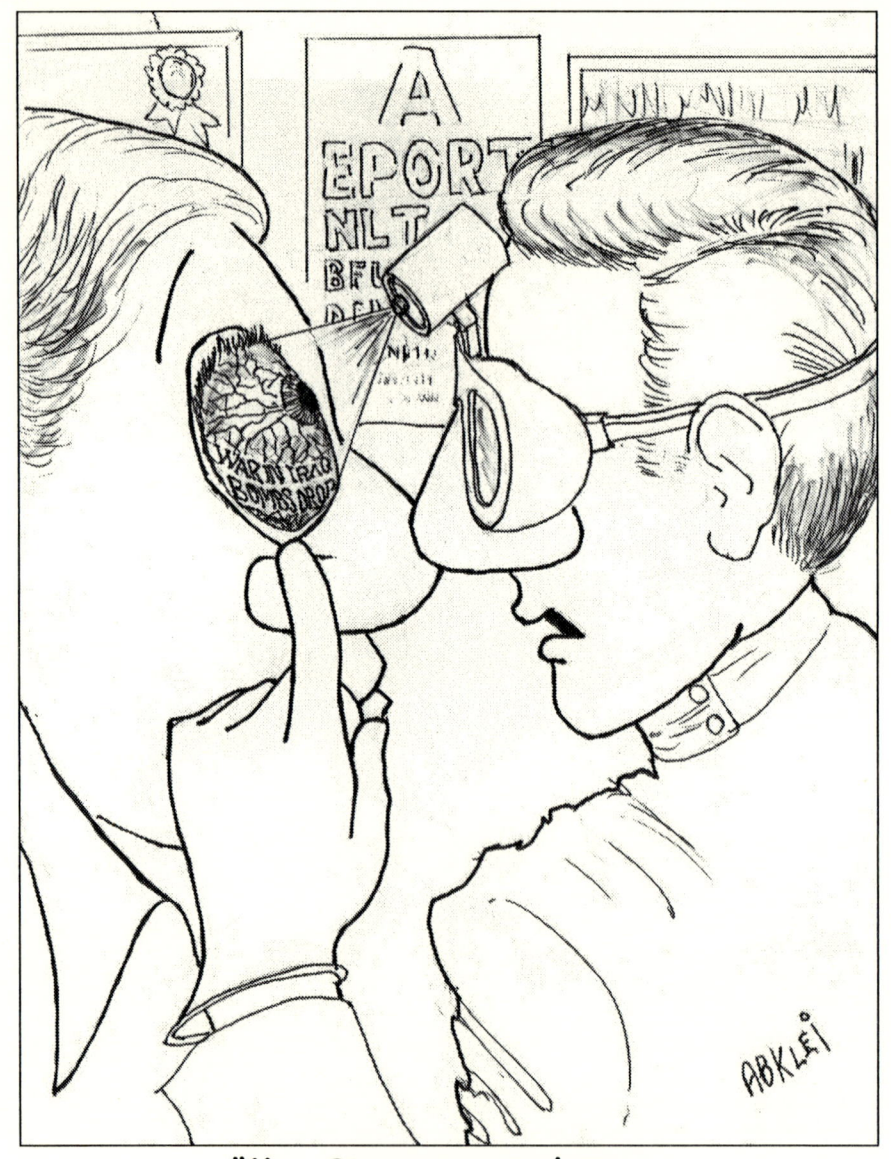

"Mr. Stewart, you have a severe case of CNNitis."

In the Beginning There Was Laughter

"HOW ABOUT CARPET BOMBING?"

Abe Kleiman

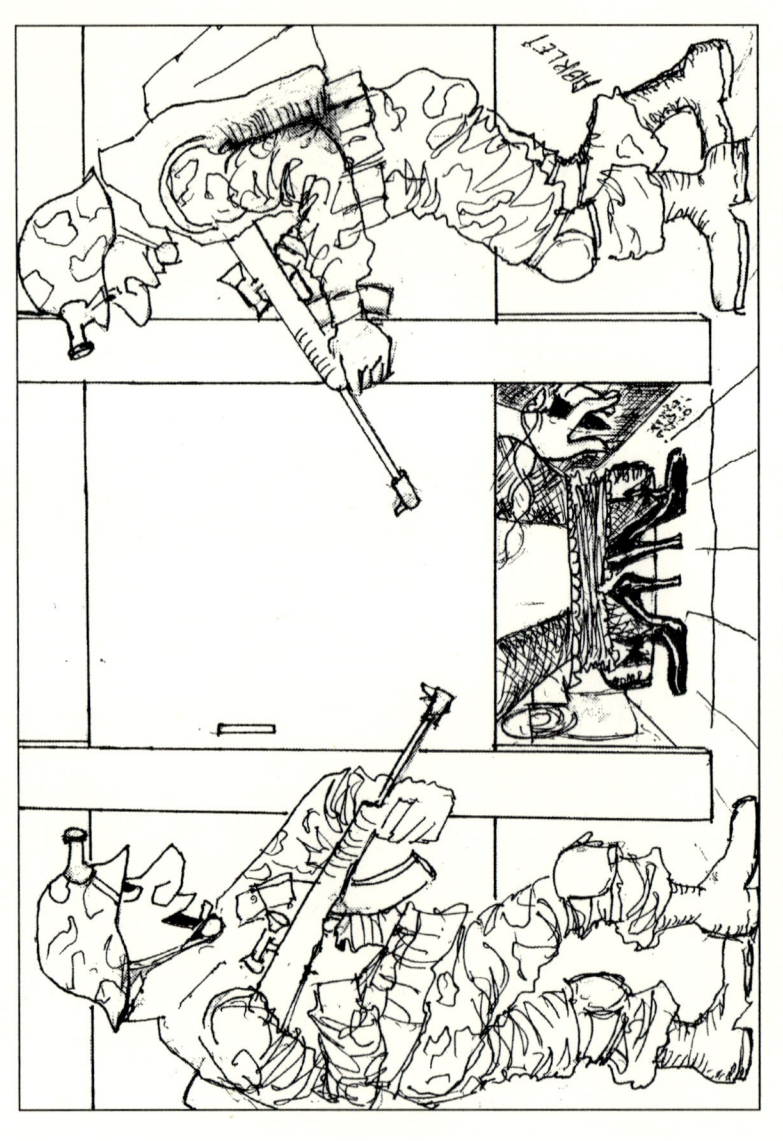

"OK Saddam! We know you are in there!"

In the Beginning There Was Laughter

"She is always striving to be the center of attention."

Abe Kleiman

"Will you kindly tell the person in 4A to stop following me?"

In the Beginning There Was Laughter

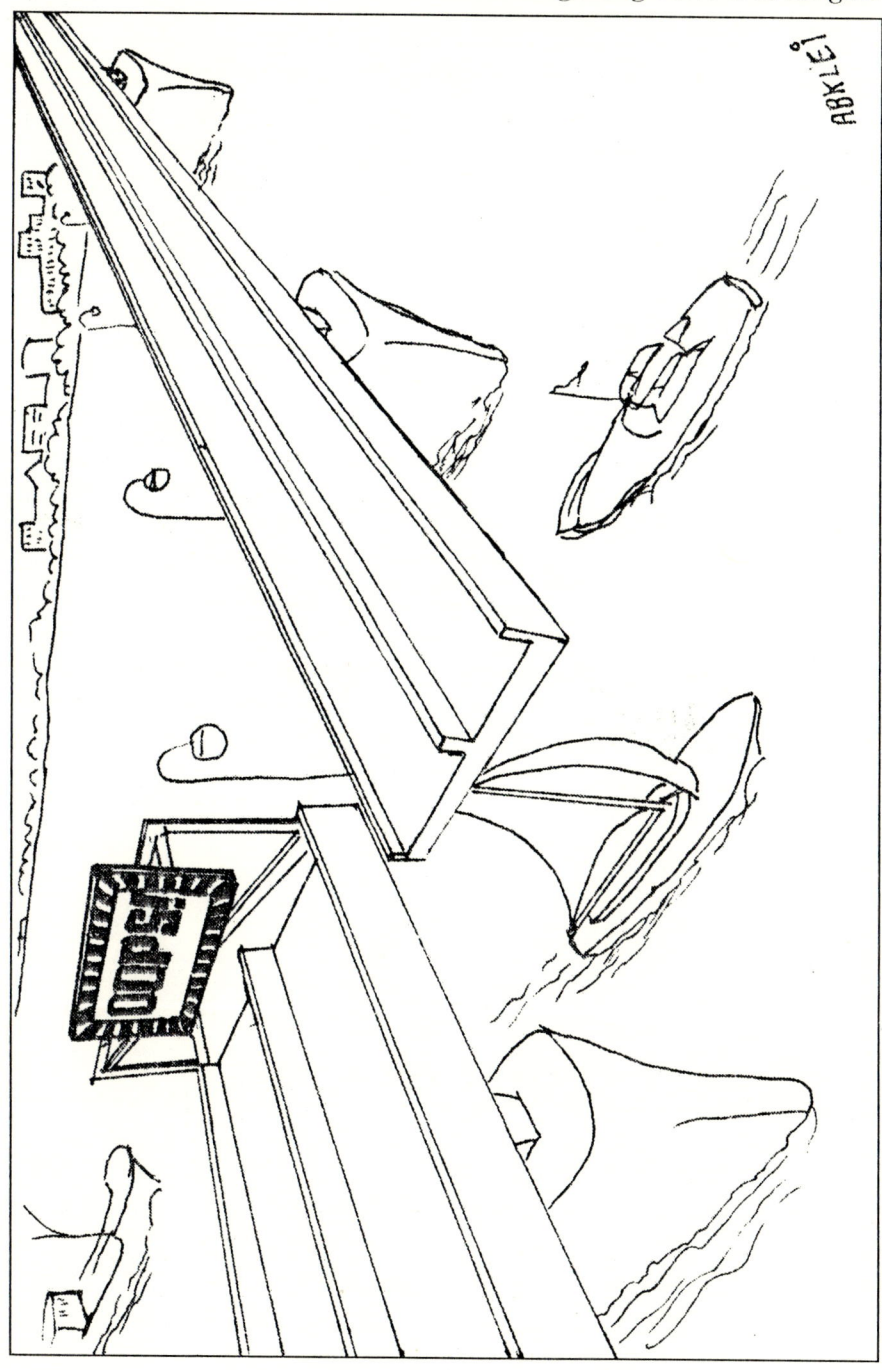

Abe Kleiman

"Dr. Sloan, can I see this on instant replay?"

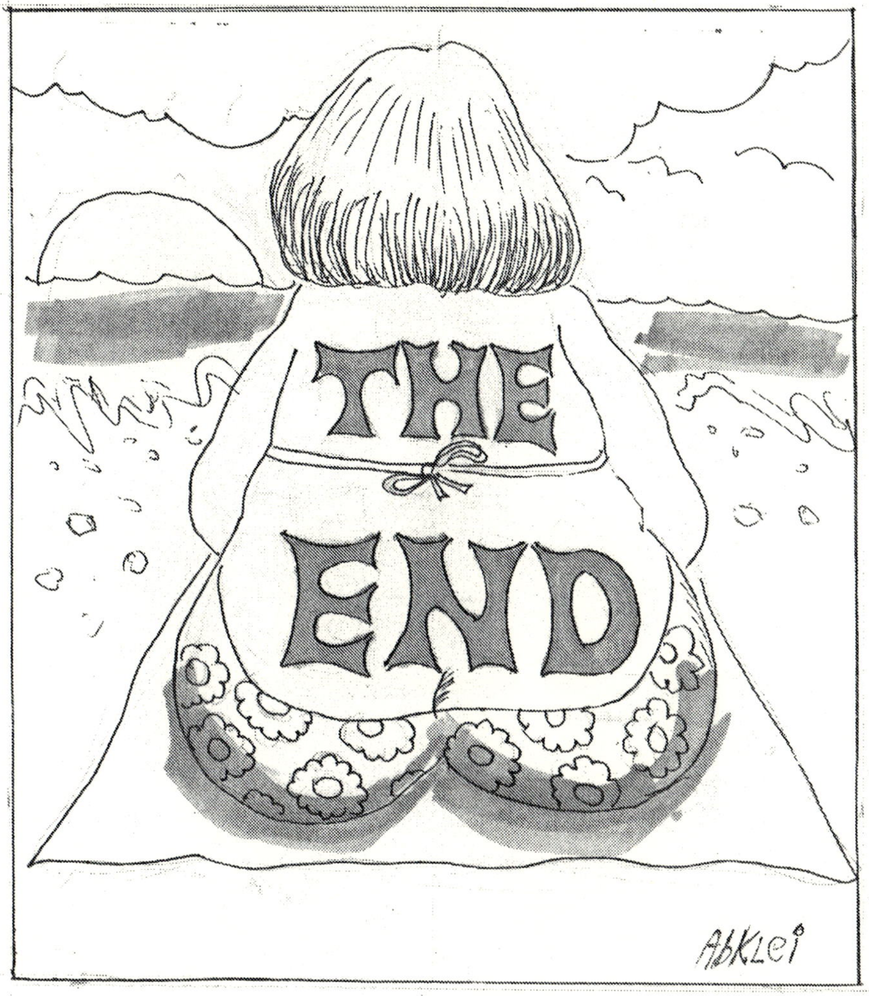
THE
END
AbKlei

Printed in the United States
16333LVS00006B/73-102